From Muddy Water

From Muddy Water

Allan Davis

IGUANA

Publisher: Meghan Behse
Editor: Toby Keymer
Front cover design: Ruth Dwight, designplayground.ca

ISBN 978-177180-523-0 (paperback)
ISBN 978-177180-524-7 (ebook)

This is an original print edition of *From Muddy Water*.

Prologue

The twelve-room Victorian red-brick mansion on Brunswick Avenue, built in 1880 by a wealthy lumber broker, had been sold in 1960 to Dr. Gabriel Lazore, chief of staff at the Provincial Mental Hospital at 999 Queen Street East in Toronto. Dr. Lazore, whose hobby was experimenting with electrical gadgets, had invented a home-use blood pressure monitor to be used by his obese wife, who had a heart condition. He had also perfected a timing device for cameras that allowed him to take pictures of his family with him included. His favourite pose centred Mrs. Lazore in a high-backed chair, with the baby, Isabela, in her lap. He would stand behind the chair with nine-year-old Gabriella, deathly pale and thin as an empty dress, on his left. These photos he framed and hung in the living room and dining room and along the lower and upper hallways of the Lazore mansion.

Dr. Lazore also invented a battery small enough to fit into a doll for Gabriella. The doll cried when Gabriella laid it down and stopped when she picked it up and rocked it. The doctor, who worked long hours at the asylum, didn't realize that when the rocking motion would not quiet the doll's annoying screech, Gabriella would smack the doll's head with her open palm until it fell silent. When she could not silence the racket with a smack, she beat the doll with her fist. When this did not work, she would take it into the basement, a spooky place with empty rooms and damp hallways filled with hollow noises, and bash the doll's head against the stone foundation until the crying stopped.

The baby Isabela developed colic soon after her birth. She cried day and night. Mrs. Lazore paced from kitchen to dining room to living room to library, rocking and swaying the baby, humming a lullaby until the child fell asleep. But no sooner did Mrs. Lazore put Isabela down than the wailing resumed. This continued night after night until one hot June day in 1969, Mrs. Lazore collapsed from exhaustion. Gabriella, tired of the wailing, carried her baby sister into the basement and beat her head against the wall until the crying stopped. When Mrs. Lazore regained consciousness later that afternoon, she found Gabriella playing quietly with her doll, her dress spattered with blood. Fearing Gabriella would be locked up for life, either in 999 Queen Street or the Whitby Psychiatric Hospital, Mrs. Lazore took the blame. She told her husband that the baby's non-stop screeching had caused her mind to snap. He believed her. He pick-axed a hole in the concrete floor of the basement and buried the infant under three inches of cement.

That night Dr. Lazore helped his wife pack a few belongings into their car. He drew her a map with instructions to his sister's house in Montreal. After Mrs. Lazore left, he informed the neighbours and his employer that the death of his wealthy father-in-law had necessitated his immediate return to Montreal to settle an estate worth millions, his wife being the sole benefactor. He implied he might not need to return.

The Brunswick Avenue mansion sat abandoned until, on January 4, 1990, the city was notified by the law firm of Williams and Smith that Dr. Lazore had died, followed shortly by Mrs. Lazore.

Mrs. Lazore stated in her will that the house should go to the provincial government to be used as a family-style home for mentally challenged adults. She specified that the province was to erect a statue of the doctor to stand on an eight-foot square slab next to the front walk. She asked that, to protect this monument against vandals, the province erect a black iron fence around the property.

The stonemason hired to design the statue, Arnie Lenssen, worked from a photograph of Dr. Lazore and Gabriella standing side by side, but confusion with names — Gabriel or Gabriella? — resulted in Mr. Lenssen carving the wrong subject. The workmen erected a statue of Gabriella — not the doctor — in a shady spot in the side yard, well back but visible from the protective iron fence running along the front of the property.

No one noticed or cared about the mix-up.

Heritage property designations in the city prevented the Lazore mansion from being turned into a group home, so it sat deserted for years. Gabriella's statue stood in the shadows, watching neighbours come and go. Rumours about the spooky property grew. Long-time residents admitted they had not known the family well, but the former owner of the Pilot Tavern on Bloor Street remembered Dr. Lazore as a slight man with thinning hair who sometimes stopped by after his shift at the Queen Street facility to fortify himself before returning home to a crying baby, a strange daughter, and a neurotic wife who outweighed the doctor by a hundred pounds. According to the tavern's owner, now in a retirement home, Gabriella, white-faced, pale-eyed, and skeletal-thin, was a mental case. Add the three hundred pounds of jiggling fat mother and that crying baby, and it was plain to see that the poor doctor had been in a nasty situation.

The owner of Betty's Quick Cuts on Bloor Street said her mother, now dead, had lived in the house behind the Lazore mansion at 220 Howland. She had gotten so accustomed to the crying child that when she stopped hearing it one day, she wondered what was different and looked over the back fence in time to see Dr. Lazore open the hurricane doors leading to the basement and disappear inside. The next day, the family was gone. "My mother's opinion," said Betty to her clients, "is that story about inheriting millions was baloney. That baby Isabela is buried somewhere on the Lazore property, and that weird statue is Gabriella, come back in a different form to make certain that wailing baby stays buried."

Speculations by neighbours were not a good enough reason for the police to dig for anything suspicious. Most of the original neighbours moved away or died. The new faces that took their place complained to the city that the property was an eyesore and should be torn down. The Historical Society argued that it should be renovated as an historic site.

Unfortunately, the city had no money for such renovations. Not until the spring of 2000, with the help of the law firm Carson and Cranks, did the city manage to sell what was now known as *the Lazore* to a Mr. Chong, a Chinese real-estate speculator who wanted to knock it down and build condos.

Approval for demolition was blocked by the Historical Society, and Mr. Chong bankrupted himself through fruitless litigation. The Lazore, a decrepit blight on the affluent neighbourhood, awaited its fate, which arrived on June 15, 2017, when the first of the three little neighbourhood girls went missing.

Chapter One

My last case as a homicide detective had been Jesse Boxer, found not guilty for the attempted murder of his wife, Elizabeth. His defense attorney explained that Jesse had a collection of antique books, some as heavy as boulders, lined up alphabetically on shelves on his home office wall. Jesse was on a stool, reaching for one of the heaviest, when he lost his balance, flung his arm backward, and unintentionally slammed the book across the back of his wife's head, putting her in a permanent coma. He had never meant to harm her.

According to Jesse's daughter, he had climbed down from the stool and slammed the book sideways into her mother's head, 100% intentionally. He said, she said, Jesse walked, bullshit from start to finish.

My second-last case began on a bridge over the Speed River. It was a late April evening, almost dark. This guy's name was Mario, a repeat offender I knew well. The missing tail light gave me a reason to pull Mario over on the bridge to see what he was up to. As I stepped out of my unmarked, Mario opened the rear door of his Honda and lifted out a baby dressed in a pink bonnet and snuggy. He stood by the rail, gently rocking the infant, watching me approach.

"I thought that might be you, Mario. How's things going?"

Mario standing so close to the railing with the baby was making me nervous. "Is that your new baby, Mario?"

"Not my baby, Detective Quinn. It belongs to my wife. She won't be needing it anymore."

Mario appeared calm. The Honda was idling away the seconds. The baby stared with blue-eyed innocence. But as I got closer, I saw that Mario's eyes, also blue, were glassed over, either from drinking or from drugs, and he was not hugging the baby but holding it at waist level, like a basketball.

"Boy or girl, Mario? Dumb question. Girls get dressed in pink. I love babies. I never had any of my own." I forced a chuckle, attempting to relax the situation. "None that I know of, anyway. But you never know. You hear stories about a daughter arriving on the father's doorstep saying, guess what?"

Mario's blank blue stare told me that Mario was not interested in a pleasant chat.

"Can I have a peek? Looks like her dad, I bet." The moment I said this, I knew that I had tripped a breaker in Mario's brain.

"I think you should put her back in the car, Mario." I stepped close enough that I could grab the baby. But I didn't. I opened the car door and stepped aside to give Mario the chance to put the baby back into its seat.

"It belongs to my wife, and I just put *her* in a dumpster. I was taking the kid to my sister. I'd be almost there by now. But you stopping me has pissed me off."

Mario swung the baby sidearm. Too late, I lunged for the child. She arced into the cool night air and dropped thirty yards to the river. I scrambled down the embankment to the water's edge, where I watched the baby disappear into the muddy spring runoff.

Mario's lawyer was going to use the "crime of passion" defense. His star witness would be the private detective hired by Mario to follow the wife and document her numerous affairs. I knew the jury wouldn't buy it. I hoped Mario would get life, exactly what he deserved. That should have been the extent of my thinking about this case.

But that baby flying through the air triggered something in my brain. The pink bonnet disappearing into the swirling river mud triggered something in my emotions. The fact that I hadn't jumped in to save the child triggered something in my mind. Added to that was the probability that if I hadn't stopped Mario for the missing tail light, that baby would still be alive. Added to that, was the realization that if I'd grabbed the baby instead of opening the car door...

The chief asked, "Can you swim, Detective Quinn?"

"No, I can't."

"Then all you have to do is change the picture in your mind from 'brown water swallowing pink baby' to 'man on bank can't swim.'"

"It's not that easy."

"Then take a few months off and go to therapy. This case was unusual, not like shooting someone who needed to be dead."

My partner, Parsons, said, "You protect yourself. You shoot before you get shot. You don't jump in if you can't swim. You make the stop because that's your job. You make split-second decisions because you have no choice. That's how the system works. You don't second guess yourself. Otherwise, the system stops working."

"Nevertheless," I replied to Parsons, "something happens that points you in a direction and you take it. Maybe you catch the baby before she hits the water and maybe you don't. But I don't want to face that situation again."

"You're only forty-three, too young to retire. Take a leave of absence and get your batteries recharged."

But to me it was more than that. My batteries were low, yes, but my tires had been flattened. What it felt like was I was in the ditch, out of gas. So, in a nice ceremony at 54 Division on June 1, 2020, I got my police retirement ring, and that was that.

Up to that point, I hadn't been much of a thinker. Parsons was the thinker. Parsons was a details person. No stone unturned and all that. He had eyes in the back of his head. He could see around corners. I was the muscle, the heavy, the deterrent. We made a great team. I would miss the team part.

"So, what will you do?" asked Parsons.

We were having a few beers at Sailor's.

"I've been thinking about Mario's private detective. Cheating spouses seems like a good business to get into. It's a popular pastime for almost everyone, really catching on, like doing yoga with goats."

Soon afterward, I found myself a small storefront office on Dupont Street and advertised myself as Quinn and Associates, specialists in tracking marital infidelities.

For two months, I sat alone in my office waiting for the phone to ring. No clients meant no associates. Recently divorced, I sat alone in my living room, no wife to talk to. I had no family. All this added to the nightmares I was having about the drowned baby, specifically the one about the child screaming in her high, thin voice from the well's darkness as the bucket I had put her in disappeared down the hole. This nightmare began to stir up a series of regrets about not having children, about having missed the father/baby friends drop around to bring cutesy presents and say "ooh" and "aah" to the new daughter in her pink booties and bonnet. No daughter meant no piano recitals, no graduation celebrations, no one to bring joy and comfort in my old age. Yeah, I know. I was feeling sorry for myself.

The quickest route from my detached on Palmerston to my Quinn and Associates office on Dupont was along Brunswick. One late-June morning, I stopped my car to help a woman driving a Hyundai SUV change her flat tire.

"It was probably flattened by one of those ghosts," she said, holding my suit jacket while I removed the flat.

"Ghosts?"

She pointed to the Lazore house. "Number 208." She smiled. "I shouldn't be judgmental."

"Why? Not politically correct to say anything against ghosts? I'm sure they're all model ghosts in there."

I hefted the spare onto the studs.

She said, "I hope I'm not making you late for work."

"I'm a private detective, nothing pressing this morning."

She pointed again to the Lazore. "I think with that statue of the little girl Gabriella staring at you it looks like the graveyard of those three little girls."

I shook my head. "Homicide investigated the Lazore when each of the three children in this area went missing. No connection. And remember, the police charged the Colombian nanny. She's serving life in Millhaven."

"Yes, but police never found their bodies." And then she asked, "Were you on the case?"

"Me? No. I worked vice. I had nothing to do with it. But my former partner, Parsons, was. After the third missing girl he insisted the yard be searched using ground-penetrating radar. The Lazore is an old house, sure, but not in any way haunted, and no buried bodies."

The lady peered at me. "Take another look at your surroundings, Detective. Tell me what you see."

I looked. Brunswick Avenue was lined with trees, and most of the houses were well cared for. But I had to admit that the falling-apart mansion, set back in the shadows with its sagging gutters and clouded windows and peeling paint, did look haunted, especially with the statue of that little girl staring out of the gloom at passersby.

The woman said, "I visited that museum in Elora that used to be the Institute for the Feeble-Minded. It sits up on a hill. Every time I pass the Lazore I think of that place. People walking by late at night have seen ghosts in there. I believe whoever took the children is in there. And I think they're buried next to that statue."

"Those cases are closed. The nanny, I don't recall her name, was working for the Medellín Cartel. She's locked up for three life terms. That's about all I remember."

I finished ratcheting the tire and straightened up. I appraised the woman for sanity: middle-aged, neatly dressed in a plain blouse and straight-leg pants similar to my ex-wife's entire wardrobe. She looked normal. But so did my ex-wife.

I said, "There have been lots of stories about the Lazore, they come and they go. But they're just stories."

I wiped my hands with a rag from under the front seat of my Toyota.

"You mentioned you're a private detective. Could I have your card?"

I obliged, wished the woman a good day, and went on my way. The next day I received a call from Rachelle Collins thanking me again for helping with the tire. "I belong to the Shepherd Foundation, a volunteer organization dedicated to finding missing children after the police have given up or the parents are convinced the police got the wrong person. I'm representing the parents in the Brunswick Avenue neighbourhood. Those three little girls, five, six and seven, each went missing *this* time of year, the first three years ago, and the second two years ago, and the third last year. You said your partner worked the case. We're wondering if you could persuade the police to reopen the files."

My response was immediate. "Parsons was very thorough. They've got their man, or, in this case, woman, so no, not a chance."

"You're a private detective. You do your own investigating. We can pay."

"You'd be wasting your money."

"What if I told you that, having talked to the parents of the three little girls, we discovered they all had one thing in common: a Filipino nanny, not a Colombian one."

"I don't know anything about that. But I'm sure Parsons wouldn't have missed that fact."

"Yes, and I have researched the involvement of nannies in hundreds of cold-case child abductions, none of them Filipino."

The woman's persistence reminded me of my pushy, anal ex-wife. I answered in a slow, firm voice. "I am sorry, ma'am. I'm sure you will find someone who will help you, but that someone is not me."

"What if I remind you they each disappeared in June, right around this time? If we're right, and the nanny isn't guilty, another child could go missing soon. What if I say we can give you a generous contract?"

"I'm sorry."

At that point, she appeared to give up. We said polite goodbyes, and I hung up. That should have been the end of it. But my next call was from Parsons to tell me the police had stopped looking for the body of Mario's baby. I pictured my own little girl, if I'd had one, disappearing into some muddy hole never to be seen again, except every single night in my nightmares — a haunting thought.

The next morning, as I drove along Brunswick to my office, my eyes were drawn to the Lazore house. From there, they were drawn to the statue of Gabriella. Hidden in the shadows of the early morning's clouds, the statue's eyes caught mine on the way by. They seemed to be inviting me to stop at the gate and come into the yard for a closer look. Then, on the way home, those same eyes in the glints of late-evening sunlight somehow cast an ominous warning for me to stay away.

I am not superstitious and do not believe in anything I can't touch. But now each time I passed the property, a vague *I wonder if they've got the right nanny in jail* repeated itself in my mind, causing me to slow down as Gabriella caught me in her line of sight, casting a haunt on me in the form of the words I'd read in a recent late-night Google search: in the summer heat, the Speed River is a shallow trickle. During the spring run-off, the water is less than two feet deep, barely up to your knees.

So now, added to the recurring "I wonders" and "if onlys" and the fact that the rushing water was barely over my ankles was the question: how many "if onlys" and how many "I wonders" must those parents be continually wading through in their late-night dreams?

Before the Mario incident, I would have said that what that chunk of cement fashioned by chisel and hammer seemed to be was pretty much all there was. Before the Mario incident, I would have said, If that statue is giving you the creeps, drive a different route.

But here I was seated at my laptop reading from newspaper write-ups the facts of the "Three Little Girls": the first, Linda, home from a school with a cold, had been playing in the fenced-in backyard while the nanny was doing the vacuuming. The second, Madeline, seven, was also home from school, playing in the backyard while the nanny was upstairs. The third, Shelley, also home from school playing in the backyard, disappeared while the nanny was on the phone. In other words, the same pattern with the same nanny. But also the same pattern for thousands of nannies on a sunny afternoon of a June day.

Well, maybe. But I didn't want to add other people's guilt to my own. And I definitely did not want to jeopardize my friendship with Parsons by poking about in a case he had solved. If the parents were determined, they would hire someone else to right the wrong nanny, if indeed she was the wrong nanny.

Chapter Two

A woman with a little girl who looked about five had moved into the house next door, 222 Howland Street, between Lois's house and the one with those two yappy dogs. They made as much noise as the roofers on her other side. Lois thought, Let's hope that little girl isn't another cry baby. When will there be any peace and quiet around here?

From her living room window, Lois had watched the men from Cross Country Movers carry out the furniture of the former owner. The next day, Lois had watched the Atlas Movers back into the front yard, almost blocking off the street. She had watched a collection of shabby-looking items being carried in by three shabby-looking men.

The day after that, Lois had watched the little girl, a cute little thing with blonde pigtails that swung back and forth as she rode her tricycle up and down the front walk. So far, no sign of a man, in other words, a father, assuming the woman was the mother.

Within a day or two, Lois had noticed that the mother was not good about supervising, other than to come out on the front step from time to time to call, "Emily, are you all right?"

The following Monday morning a squat Latina woman arrived. The nanny, Lois decided. The mother left a few minutes later in her red Focus parked across the street. On the fifth day there was still no sign of a father, but definite signs of a pattern. At eight o'clock, the dumpy nanny arrived on short legs in flat shoes. At eight-twenty, the mother, wearing an office-type skirt and top and matching low-heeled shoes, left for work. Emily came out just after nine-thirty to ride her tricycle in the early June sunshine. At ten-thirty, the nanny called for Emily to come in, perhaps to have a snack. From eleven to twelve, Emily played with her dolls in the grass of the backyard. At twelve, the nanny called her in for lunch. Lois would not see Emily again until after three, when she would play with her shovel and bucket in the sandbox.

On Saturday morning the mother, wearing tight jeans and a T-shirt, stood on the back stoop and called, "Emily, time to go." Hand in hand, they walked across the front lawn to the red Focus. An hour later, they returned. The mother unbuckled Emily and they disappeared into the house with their shopping. After about ten minutes, Emily came out to ride her tricycle. She was wearing a new green-and-yellow jacket over her blue dress with blue socks and black shoes with a buckle strap. The buckle strap reminded Lois of when she was a little girl riding her tricycle on the sidewalk in front of the house now called the Lazore.

Lois enjoyed singing each Sunday morning in the Seniors' Church Choir. Her favourite hymn from when she was little growing up in the Lazore was "What a Friend We Have in Jesus." Her volunteer work at the Oxford Nursing Home was depressing, but she did it because it was her Christian duty. Her investment account established by her father, Dr. Lazore, did not provide enough money to pay her living expenses, so she took in sewing.

Lois knew that when she died, the service would be conducted by Reverend Beachy. All her acquaintances from church would come to her pre-paid funeral to say to one another what a tragedy it was to lose such a nice person, not one of them realizing that, as a child named Gabriella, she had bashed her baby sister's brains out — noisy little creature — in the basement of the Lazore. Or that Isabela was still there, in fact.

Being a single woman, Lois had been forced to learn enough basic household maintenance skills to be able to seal off a room in the basement of her house, 220 Howland. She had soundproofed the walls with R12 insulation between the two-by-four studs. Using extension cords, she had installed lights over her workbench where she made rag dolls of cotton and silk. All of them were hand-sewn. Their hair of wool was fastened tight with her glue gun. The dolls were neatly lined up on a shelf along one wall.

Instead of making rag dolls, she sometimes asked herself, why not sew clothing for the poor starving African children the church ladies raised money for? No, the answer came to her. She shouldn't care about African children, but about her dolls, each one stitched to perfection and finished with a name inscribed in tiny letters on the belly button: Isabela.

And, she said to herself, why not sell her dolls at the market like you might mitts or scarves and make a little profit? Or to a gallery to achieve fame as an artist? No, the answer came to her. She should not make her dolls for fame or profit. Besides, they were all the same and all called Isabela.

Mind you, Lois did not hear these answers in distinct words because the insulation prevented any voice from above from being heard in the basement workroom below. But an answer came to her nevertheless: "These dolls are not to be taken to any market or to any gallery, like Inuit carvings of birds or fish. Agreed, they would be a good investment for collectors; although each one is the same, each one is unique. Buyers would request special orders, knowing that when the artist died, there would be no more Isabelas. But no, shame on you, Gabriella. You cannot sell your baby sister."

Lois talked to her Isabelas. To each, she whispered her secrets as she molded the little fingers and sewed the happy faces. But sometimes a smiley face would turn into a frown, perhaps from colic caused by breathing the fumes from the glue gun. When this little Isabela started the nonstop wailing, Lois's mind would become addled, and her brain would turn itself so far off the dial that all Lois would hear morning till night was the constant static of the screaming baby. So, having no choice, Lois would bash this little Isabela against the basement wall until it stopped. Noisy little creature didn't matter. She had lots more Isabelas.

One Sunday, she asked Reverend Beachy, "Would you perform the funeral service for my doll?"

When he laughed at her, she regretted the conversation and began to fear that in his prayers to God, Reverend Beachy would mention that something was not right with Lois. He wouldn't mention her name, of course. That would be confidential. But the problem was, she doubted Reverend Beachy would realize that an all-knowing, all-seeing God wouldn't need a name.

Lois imagined the fireworks display that would happen if God decided he was no longer in favour of what she was doing with her dolls. God could change his mind any time he wanted. He would instruct her to put on her choir gown, sing a hymn, say a prayer and spark the match and ignite the glue fumes and blow the place up, and her along with it.

She asked Reverend Beachy, "Does God want me to make rag dolls?"

"I'm sure God doesn't mind."

"If he did mind, would he blow up the house with me in it? After all, he sent plagues and floods to punish his people when they were doing things he didn't like."

"Yes, but that was the judgmental Old Testament God. The Christian, loving God would do no such thing. Besides, there is nothing wrong with making rag dolls if that's what you like to do."

One problem remained. The bashed-in little creatures lying in their little deathbeds did not look plastic or waxy like people laid out in coffins. The Isabelas looked pretty much the same as when they were sleeping. One time, at a funeral for one of the churchwomen, Lois said to Reverend Beachy, "If one of my dolls dies, how will it know if it's dead or sleeping?"

Reverend Beachy looked at her strangely and asked, "Are you feeling all right, Lois?"

"I feel fine. But you know, say someone falls asleep and has a stroke and never wakes up. How does that person know if he or she is dead or still asleep?"

Reverend Beachy had concern in his eyes. "Is this a spiritual question, Lois?"

Lois thought it was.

"That is why we have funerals, Lois."

"But not for dolls," she said.

"I heard there is a Baptist minister in Tennessee who does funerals and weddings for dogs."

Lois brightened. "Would he do dolls, do you think?"

"I'm sure he would do anything for the right price, but Tennessee is a long way away."

Lois decided to sew a rag doll priest to perform the funerals. Then she sewed a rag doll undertaker. He fixed each dead Isabela up to look nice and dead in a pink sleeper and matching bonnet. He arranged a nice service with the priest. On the day of each funeral, Lois wore a gold chain with a tiny crucifix, bought at the Christian supplies store, on sale because the cross was upside down. After the funeral, she told the undertaker and the priest, "I want you to open the hurricane doors into the Lazore basement and jackhammer a hole in the Lazore floor and lay each Isabela to rest. That way, even if they're sleeping, they can't come back to drive me crazy with their crying."

But the undertaker asked her, "Is it wise to jackhammer a hole into the floor? Won't everyone hear it?"

She decided to bury the dead dolls next to her statue. This proved inconvenient, however, for she had to do the digging under the cover of darkness, and in the winter, there could be no digging. But that was the best she could do for now. The truth was, according to the church organist who worked at City Hall, they would soon be selling the property cheap. Lois would sell her house, buy back the Lazore, and dig up those three Isabelas buried under the statue and entomb each one, Linda, Madeline, and Shelley, in the basement next to Isabela where they belonged.

Lois had never thought of any child playing with one of these rag dolls. But then, when that little girl named Linda moved in down the street, Lois invited her into the kitchen to play with

Isabela. She first asked permission from the nanny, of course. The little girl had sat at the table with Isabela in her lap and Lois had served tea in little teacups like the church women at the Ladies Aid meetings. Lois had enjoyed the sisterly look on Linda's face as Lois demonstrated the correct way to rock Isabela if she started to cry.

Then, a problem. When Linda started to fuss and cry and wail, Lois decided she needed some rocking. But that was not easy because this little girl wasn't a baby and wasn't little. She was heavy. Fat, in fact. A little porker. Lois already had back problems from carrying the lumber to install her workshop. She had heard on the news that auto workers weren't allowed to lift anything heavier than thirty-five pounds. This little girl was heavier than that.

Under the yellow-and-green jacket, Emily wore a blue dress with blue socks and black shoes, reminding Lois of when she was a little girl, riding her tricycle on the sidewalk in front of the house now called the Lazore.

Chapter Three

The payout to my ex-wife was eating up half my early-retirement pension. To help with the bills until I got some contracts, I converted the top floor of my detached to a one-bedroom apartment, an easy fix because the front door of the house opened to a vestibule, the stairs to the left, my living room to the right, my kitchen straight ahead. Shut the living room and kitchen door and the two units were private, each with its own bathroom. Parsons and I installed a small kitchen in the upper unit using Ikea pre-fab kits. To avoid the expense of wiring in a stove, I decided a microwave would do.

I intended to rent the upstairs furnished to a single gentleman who would cook frozen dinners, pay the rent on time, come home at a decent hour, quietly climb the stairs, and mind his own business. Instead, maybe because there was no stove, I had to take the only applicant who wanted it. Kirsten was a brunette twenty-something waitress at the Double Deuce Tavern on Bloor Street. She looked too young to be reliable — her party-girl style of tight top and distressed jeans suggested boyfriends all hours of the day and night — but having spent the time and the money on the renovation, I was desperate.

She couldn't afford first and last, so I accepted her promise to pay by the end of the week. The day after she moved in, Kirsten tapped on my living room door. "Would it be okay if I watched *Duck Dynasty* on your television until mine gets hooked up?"

I was in and out all day long, so it seemed okay to unlock my part of the house. "Just you, no friends," I said.

By the end of her first week, she was wandering in before or after her afternoon bar shift at the Double Deuce to both watch my television and borrow my *Toronto Star* to read her horoscope.

"What sort of detecting do you do?" She was slouched on her spine on my chesterfield, fiddling with some kind of locket on a chain. She was wearing a tight black T-shirt and faded low-rise jeans that showed her bare midriff.

"Cheating spouses."

"That's it?"

"My specialty." I handed her a business card.

"This says 'Quinn and Associates.'"

"No associates. Just me. But I plan to expand."

"Why cheaters?"

"Easy work that pays well. My clients are all from high-end postal codes: doctors, lawyers."

In fact, I had only one client, a deal I had made with the plumber who had helped with the kitchen.

"What cheater are you working on now?"

"His name is Larry. He had no idea that the wife was cheating until he got a summons in the mail for an unpaid parking ticket. Both the cars were in his name. He didn't think anything about it, didn't mention it to the wife, and paid the ticket, thinking, you know, she was shopping, the meter ran out, whatever. Then he got another one for the same address. Same response, he paid the ticket. With the third one, he drove to the address. It was a private residence."

"I know the story. I work in a bar. Cry me a river."

I said, "There are two kinds of husbands: the ones who believe the wife would never cheat, even when she is, and the ones who believe the wife *would* cheat, even when she isn't."

This seemed like a nice answer to give when asked the question I would probably get regularly asked.

"May I make a comment?" She sat up to fasten the locket thing around her neck.

"Please do."

"You say 'the wife' like you would say 'the dog' or 'the refrigerator.'"

Uh-oh. One of those. "A detective needs to be objective."

"So, in your objective opinion, as far as the cheated are concerned, cheating or not cheating is about belief and not about truth."

This way of saying it was a bit abstract for me, but yes, that was the drift of what I was saying. "If you don't know and don't find out, it didn't happen."

"You should put that on your card. 'Happy is the one whose eyes are never opened because, once they are, they can never be closed.' I think that's from the I Ching."

Mention of the I Ching reminded me of a stripper I'd known when I worked vice. Her real name was Carmen. She drank weird tea and wore bracelets that kept away evil spirits and quoted the I Ching.

Kirsten said, "Three things cannot be long hidden: the sun, the moon, and the truth. The sun and the moon love to show themselves. The truth loves to hide. That's Buddha, or the I Ching, you know, in the part where they throw the bones to divine the future."

This barmaid is getting strange, I thought.

She said, "When you find out cheating is going on, you should give the cheater a chance to stop before you turn him in. You could help him patch things up."

"You assumed 'he.' So far, my cheaters have all been women."

"Then they probably had good reason."

"Not from what I've seen." I tried to sound like I had been tracking cheaters for years. "Most relationships are destined for failure the minute they start. But no one seems capable of seeing the cracks until they turn into canyons."

"That's because it's not about what's actually happening in reality but about what's going on in your mind. You start thinking about something and then your mind gets busy with it, and you start finding clues to support what you're thinking, and pretty soon your thoughts become truth."

"Hmm. Funny you should mention that. What's been going on in my mind, I mean, what made me retire…" And I told her about the missing little girls and Mario's baby and told her the Lazore story and told her that the Gabriella statue was now somehow casting a spell on me and, I don't know, once I got started I couldn't stop.

"What is the nature of this spell?"

I hesitated, embarrassed to tell her about my dream. "There's a bucket sitting on the edge of a stone well with a large iron crank. From the rattle of the bucket and the grating of the crank and the blackness of the well, the child in the bucket becomes frightened and begins to scream as the bucket disappears down the hole. So, I grab the rope, not bothering with the crank, and in the bucket, up comes a baby."

She gave me a questioning look. "Could it be, Detective, that there was another baby in your life that you should have saved?"

I did not have to think about that one. "I never had any babies."

"But you are hearing through Gabriella's statue messages from both Mario's baby and from the baby Isabela and from the missing little girls that there was another baby in your life that you left in the bucket."

I shook my head. "No, I grab the rope and pull it up."

"So this baby is around here somewhere."

"Well, it's not mine, if that's what you're getting at. I'm sterile, if you must know."

She kicked off her sandals, wrapped her arms around one pulled-up leg, one barefoot on the chesterfield, the other on the floor. She wore no makeup, at least none that I could see, and no jewelry, other than the locket thing, and was in no way looking like a therapist I would admit my impotence to. Yet, I had done just that.

She said, "Have a look into your subconscious, dude."

"It has nothing to do with my subconscious."

"Dreams have everything to do with your subconscious. You said each of the three little girls disappeared in June. Do you know someone who was born in June?"

"No one." I had no idea when anyone's birthday was.

She checked her watch, picked up the remote, and turned on *Duck Dynasty*. I checked my watch: 8:00 p.m., normally the time I watched the news.

Duck Dynasty seemed to be about a collection of bearded morons living in a swamp. As a vice cop, I had spent most of my adult life dealing with bearded morons from swamps; I did not want to watch them on television. I moved to my spare bedroom, now converted to a makeshift office with a desk/laptop/filing cabinet arrangement, leaving Kirsten slouched like a teenager on my chesterfield, now looking too young to be a barmaid and more like someone's teenage daughter.

I knew that my regret at never having a daughter was based on fantasy not reality. The daughter fantasy came from Netflix movies about daughters giving dads hugs. The daughter reality came from working vice where daughters were giving dads nervous breakdowns. Me and Parsons had investigated a racket where the services of teenage girls were sold on an internet blog called *First Date*. The ad read: "Remember your first date? This time you're guaranteed a score." I remembered the girls standing in darkened downtown doorways on cold winter nights dressed in miniskirts and heels waiting for their pickups in high-end cars. The johns, usually disgusting old men, drove to the nearest parking garage, found a secluded spot, and got cozy with their teenage date. The monetary transactions were completed by cell phone and PayPal. The pimps were in Pakistan. All the police could do was take the sixteen-year-old girls home to Daddy. They'd be back on the street in a week. A disgusting business.

The duck program ended and went to commercials, so Kirsten turned her attention to the horoscopes and I returned to my living room chair to wait for the news. I noticed her hairstyle today was the same as yesterday, a short slant cut across her forehead to hang over one eye. But her go-to-work style was different: yesterday, a jeans-and-tank-top arrangement with sandals and ankle bracelets. Today, the same, except the sandals were traded for high boots.

Now I noticed something else. She had a way of holding her hands in her lap, the red-nailed forefinger of one rubbing the thumb of the other. I was familiar with this gesture, although I had no idea why or from where.

By the end of the third week, I had become used to arriving home to find Kirsten on the chesterfield. It was a nice change after post-divorce empty evenings spent sitting in my empty easy chair listening to the lonely sounds of an empty house. But one thing was bothering me: she had not paid any rent.

One evening I came home to find her going through my CD collection. She put on a Waylon Jennings disc. When it got to, "Mammas don't let your babies grow up to be cowboys," she turned it up. I thought, Add a cowboy hat to her dance step and she could pass for a television country singer.

By the end of the fourth week, Kirsten's dress code had relaxed into a white bathrobe covered in black cats doing various tricks with cat toys. Underneath, she wore men's blue PJs, with white dogs doing various tricks with dog toys. On her bare feet, she wore cat's-face white slippers that would paddle her down the stairs and into my apartment to make a cup of musty organic tea. Then she would plunk herself down on my chesterfield in front of the TV and sip from the cup, her little finger cocked like the Queen at teatime. Her dead tea bags, looking like poisoned mice decomposing, were left in saucers on the counter of the now musty-smelling kitchen.

"Kirsten. Can I ask a question?"

"Try me."

"Why do you leave your dead tea bags that look like poisoned mice on the counter?"

She gave me a teenage-attitude scowl and got up and threw them into the garbage under the sink. She disappeared up the stairs. She returned with a deck of cards and a pack of gummy bears. She settled herself at the kitchen table and began to lay out the cards and eat the gummies.

I sat opposite her. "Kirsten. Can I ask a personal question?"

"Try me."

"How old are you?"

"I was going to ask you that same question. These are Tarot cards. What's your birthday?"

"May 5, 1973."

"What time were you born?"

"Midnight." I had no idea.

She laid three cards face-up on the table. "Your cards say you should avoid passing under power lines on your way to work."

"No kidding?" That was exactly what it felt like, being caught in the statue's — Gabriella's — powerline of sight, one minute making me want to open the gate into Dr. Lazore's past, look around, poke about, see what I might uncover, the next minute telling me to stay away, forget about it, let it rest in peace.

"Say it isn't so," said Kirsten to the card she held in her hand.

"Huh?"

"It says here you piss off everyone you come in contact with and you think most people are dickheads."

"Where does it say that?" I got up and peered over her shoulder at the card gripped by her red-nailed thumb. The picture didn't look like anything I could identify. She returned it to the deck.

"Not in those exact words."

She took another gummy bear. "Ever shoot anyone?"

"No."

"What were the birth signs of the Lazore girls, Isabela and Gabriella?"

"I don't know."

"Do you know the birth dates of the three girls who were abducted?"

"No. Not offhand."

She turned over another card. "This card says I should go with you to look at the statue."

"Why?"

She was studying the card, reading what it was telling her, it seemed. "Definitely something about babies and little girls in these cards. I see you tooling along, investigating cheaters, but your future is about a baby from the past coming into your life very soon."

"Where does it say that?"

She sighed and reshuffled the cards. "Nowhere, dude. It's not like, in a place. It's like, you Google something on your laptop and the information comes to you on the invisible wings of the internet."

I returned to my chair. "Kirsten. Can I ask you a question?"

"Try me."

I intended to say something about pajamas and bathrobe not being appropriate dress in the apartment of an older man she did not know, and perhaps suggest a less revealing dress code for going to work. But I was having trouble putting the words together in a way that would avoid her saying "keep your eyes to yourself," thereby blaming the revealing dress code problem on me. I just wanted to give her some fatherly advice. Years on vice had taught me that *suggestive* leads to *provocative* leads to *trouble. Suggestive* was the polite, politically correct word used in court when referring to the ability of young women to inflame the natural pig-dog instincts of men, especially when the young female worked in a bar.

But how Kirsten dressed was none of my business. "At eight o'clock, can I watch football on my television?"

"Sorry, dude. Eight is *Duck Dynasty*."

"How about nine?"

"Nine is *Duck Dynasty*."

"When are they going to hook up your television?"

"I don't know."

"Kirsten. Can I ask you a question?"

"Try me."

"Do you even have a television?"

Kirsten paused for another gummy bear. Apparently, this question required some thought.

She put away the cards.

"Your guilty look is telling me you don't have a television."

"I have a numerology program on my laptop. If you type in my birthday and ask me a personal question and then type in the first number that comes into your head, the computer will tell you if I'm telling the truth."

Kirsten disappeared upstairs and returned with her laptop and set it in front of me. "Type in 'June 9' and then ask me the question."

"You were born in June? What year?"

"Never mind what year. Ask me a question."

I did as told, then asked, "Do you even have a television?"

"The answer is yes. But to find out if that answer is true you have to ask me what is the first number that comes into my head."

"What is the first number that comes into your head?"

"Nine."

I typed in the number and the computer flashed a blue *True*.

"See? Works every time."

"Kirsten. Can I ask a personal question?"

"Try me."

"Why didn't you come right out and say you don't have a television?"

She crossed one leg over the other and placed her hands in her lap. The red-nailed forefinger was rubbing the thumb, the little finger cocked like the Queen at teatime. This gesture, I had learned, meant she was thinking.

"I was embarrassed. I had to pawn my television. So, yes or no would have been true. I have one but it's in the pawnshop. The tips haven't been good. Steve, the bartender, says I have to dress sexier."

"Kirsten. Are you kidding me? You already dress far too sexy."

"What's 'far too sexy?'"

"I don't know, but 'appropriate sexy' might be maybe like the beer girls at Octoberfest."

"I've never been to Octoberfest. When is it?"

"No idea."

She returned to her Tarot cards. "Oh my God." Her big questioning eyes stared at the card, her face frowning down.

"What does it say?"

"Time to stop talking and watch *Duck Dynasty*."

"What did it really say?"

"I can't tell you."

"It's all nonsense so it doesn't matter."

She said, "We'll see. Pay attention to what Kirsten says. Pay attention to the secrets being whispered in your ear by the universe, dude. You might change your tune. Talk about tune, why does a Quinn and Associates detective listen to hokey cowboy music?"

"Why does a barmaid watch the Ducks on *my* TV in *my* apartment instead of on *her* laptop in *her* apartment?"

She cocked her head. "You're right."

"About what?"

"I *should* watch the Ducks on my laptop in my own apartment."

I sat next to her on the chesterfield to watch the Ducks, trying to concentrate on this episode of nonsense about a neighbour group of hairy morons from across the swamp sitting around a long table discussing duck calls.

"They don't look like they'd be much good at trimming their hedges," I said.

"The biker guys who come into the bar look like that. Last Saturday, I poured a glass of beer on one when he tried to grab my ass."

This sparked memories of bikers I had arrested in vice, how they spit sideways when I talked to them. I imagined the pleasure I would get throwing one of these redneck duck-fuckers through the front window of the Deuce. "Are they regulars?"

"Usually, Saturday. I don't know why only Saturday. They don't have jobs. The one that grabbed my ass wears a chain around his neck."

"I'll drop by on Saturday and have a word with him."

"Don't you dare."

"Kirsten. Do you mind if I ask you a personal question?"

"Try me."

"Why don't you get a decent job?"

"Like what?"

"Like what. I don't know like what."

"None of your business."

This was true. So, not wanting to watch the Duck morons, I excused myself and went to my spare bedroom-turned-office and put on Merle Haggard while I did paperwork. At eleven, she turned off the television and disappeared upstairs. By then football was over. I watched the news and went to bed.

But I could not sleep. The Tarot cards had got me thinking about the future, as in destiny, like when you learn a buddy's got something terminal, like plaque buildup in the carotid artery that could break off any minute and leave you ninety-five per cent paralyzed. This thought, if I were younger, might have led me into reveries like, why not live a little and take advantage of the unlimited possibilities of meeting someone my age on the internet to share my television with instead of this fortune teller free-loader?

My mind skipped back to the question Kirsten had side-stepped earlier: why not watch the Ducks on your laptop? This was related to another of Kirsten's habits. I wouldn't have noticed this one if it weren't for the fact that from my chair in my bedroom office I would sometimes notice her get up from the chesterfield, refasten her bathrobe, and walk to the bathroom to check her face. Then her cat-slippered feet would pad her to the kitchen. Then I would hear her at the counter making her cup of organic tea. Then she would return to the chesterfield, sit down, and slide into her customary slouch, legs stuck out any old way under that bathrobe. There was nothing remarkable about this routine except that it seemed to be a disguise for what she really wanted to do: cup in hand, before sitting down to sip at this organic concoction like the Queen at teatime, go to the front window to pull the curtain aside and check out the street.

Parsons had been good with details, and good at reading the signs, but not me. Yet even I could pick up on the fact that she didn't watch the Ducks upstairs because she was afraid of being alone. I decided I would wait until the day she could feel my eyes on her, wait for the exact moment she would turn from the window and glance over at me and catch me watching her before asking, "Kirsten. Who are you running from?"

Chapter Four

A matronly woman with a wide face answered a knock that I had no intention of making. But after my conversation with Kirsten here I was at the door of the property next to the Lazore. "I'm the housekeeper," she answered. "If you want to see the owner, she's sleeping."

I got right to the point. "Were you working here when the three little girls went missing?"

She scowled, studying my face. Finally she admitted, "I was."

"I'm a retired police officer. My former partner, Parsons, investigated the Lazore at the time of the disappearances and reported nothing suspicious. Now, however, Rachelle Collins of the Shepherd Foundation wants me to review the case of the three missing girls."

"That case was solved. The nanny did it."

"Yes, I know. But the parents are refusing to accept that."

"Without bodies, how could they?"

I nodded. "There's much we don't know."

The woman led me into the living room, furnished with a faded blue chesterfield and two mouldy easy chairs in old lady patterns. Neither looked like I'd want to sit on them, so I stood.

She said, "The owner won't be happy about that case starting up again, if that's what you're trying to do. She's waiting for city hall to do something with that property so she can sell this property."

"And what is your connection?"

"She's an elderly lady, and I'm hired to look after her."

"Can I talk to her?"

"No, I told you, she's upstairs sleeping."

"Have you ever noticed any suspicious activity next door?"

"It's not my job to know about next door. I'm only hired to look after the old lady."

I asked, "Have you heard the stories about the Lazore?"

"I don't pay any attention to stories." She looked around, as though making sure no one was listening before she said, "But I did go one time, I shouldn't have, but I went over to peek in the windows. There are family pictures still hanging on the walls. There's one of the doctor and one of Gabriella. And one of the missus. Those were the ones I could see."

"Can you tell me anything about the family?"

She shrugged. "They vanished, left, gone, moved somewhere. But according to Ruth upstairs, Gabriella took the baby Isabela into the basement and bashed her head against the wall. They buried the baby somewhere on the property, packed up, and left."

"Did Ruth tell the police that?"

"She says she did. But she's got dementia. She says all kinds of crazy things. But I wondered if Ruth was maybe telling the truth this time. They left the pictures hanging on the wall. The first thing a woman will take with her is family pictures."

"Are they all of the Lazore family?"

"As far as I know. But I just looked in one window. And one other thing: Ruth says there's someone who comes at night to visit that statue. But she's got dementia. She says all kinds of crazy things."

"But what she says is sometimes true."

"She told me she saw Gabriella all grown up shopping in Loblaws, but I don't believe that. How would she recognize Gabriella after all these years?"

I thanked her for her time. I went next door. I cut past the statue and through the weeds of the yard to look in a side window. The dining room furniture was all there, including a picture above the chesterfield of a slight man in a suit and a goatee standing behind a fat woman sitting in a high-backed chair. Standing on one side was a thin girl in pigtails wearing a shapeless brown dress. The same chair that was in the photo was still there, sitting empty in one corner of the dining room near a glass china cabinet.

The next picture was of the same girl, same dress, legs too thin to hold up the black knee socks bunched around her brown oxfords. She was leaning against what looked like the back wall of the house.

The wood flooring of the front porch groaned as I stepped up to the front door. The groan stopped me; I didn't know why, other than I thought boards creaked, not groaned. I cupped my hands to the window. In the vestibule hung a photo of the thin girl holding a baby. For me, all babies used to look the same. I never paid much attention to them. But now, I guess because of Mario's baby, I looked closely. Isabela looked as sick as the girl holding her, Gabriella.

I stepped off the porch, blinking at the daylight. I wondered why in mid-afternoon the place seemed so dark. I stood on the front sidewalk considering the property's dreariness: the yard tall with weeds, the roofline gutters choked with leaves, the lower windows grimy with dust, and there, off to the side, staring right at me, Gabriella. She seemed to be listening to the cries of the baby Isabela seeping from the cracks in the mansion's stone foundation. I moved to the centre of the street. From this angle, she looked like she was keeping watch over the bodies of the missing girls buried in the side yard.

After the Lazore visit, I drove to Gold's Gym in Yorkdale, not to work out but to watch a banker's wife who kept a regular appointment there. I parked and waited. Her car pulled up, and ten minutes later, the trainer arrived. He was a burly character with rugged features, the opposite of her mousy husband. They did not go into the gym. I had a telephoto lens that I wasn't very good with, but exact details were not important. Their kisses and hugs upon greeting told the whole story. While the wife waited, the trainer went into a nearby Starbucks and returned with two coffees. They got into his car and left the mall. They took the Allen, me following in my Toyota, left and right, and straight up Dufferin to a Howard Johnson's, where I photographed them registering at the desk.

I delivered the photos to the waiting banker, collected my fee, and returned home to wait for Kirsten. I heard her come in the front door. I could tell she was wearing heels from the click of her steps as she climbed the stairs to her apartment. Ten minutes later, there she was in my living room in bare feet, jean shorts, and a tank top. I thought about suggesting that, if that top was how she got decent tips, she should get a different job, but she beat me to it.

"I got good tips today, most of them from a generous drunk who was having trouble with the cheating wife."

She plunked herself down on my chesterfield.

"Too bad you didn't have one of my cards," I said.

She said, "Here's what I learned: the cheated are driven to the point of insanity wondering, imagining, checking, and accusing. So, on your card, you write, 'What is the price of peace?' Then you leave a line to write in your estimate."

"The trouble is, neither the cheaters nor the cheated realize that when the evidence comes in, the war has only just begun."

"True." She nodded. "The war is just beginning. But you're giving them clarity and direction so they can get on with the fight and get the problem solved."

I liked her line of thought, and her interest in my work. "You mentioned you wanted to see the statue. We can drive over Saturday morning and have a look at the property."

"I start work at twelve."

"Then we'll go before work."

"I sleep before work."

"What if I tell you I heard whispers as I walked up to the door of that old house? I felt this sort of chill and I felt the ground get shifty. And then I heard this distinct groan, like I was stepping on a grave."

Her eyes widened, so I continued. "Then, as I studied a photo of Gabriella hanging on the wall, a voice said, 'Kirsten, who is interested in weird occult stuff and drinks weird occult tea, should have a look at this weird place.'"

Kirsten looked interested.

"The house is an old mansion with the photographs of the family still hanging on the walls, real spooky-looking. And the old lady next door says someone visits the statue, in the dead of night, looking even spookier."

Kirsten said, "I know the house and I know the Lazore story. How much will you pay me to look at the statue and check out the property?"

"Free rent for a few days."

"I'm getting free rent now."

"You're not. You owe me."

"I haven't been getting good tips."

I was getting the picture. Parsons had warned me. Once the tenant moves in, you'll never get them out, rent or no rent.

"Kirsten. Do you mind if I make a comment?"

She was lying on her spine with her bare legs straight out.

"Try me."

"You came to me homeless. Without even a television. I gave you a place to stay. But I'm not social services. You owe me."

She pretended an innocent look. "And I intend to pay you. And, if you intend to pay me, I will give you my basic checkout package. But for nothing, meaning no charge, I'll do a quick drive-by from the outside."

"A drive-by usually *is* from the outside."

She rolled her eyes. "Or, get me inside, and I'll give you my deluxe package and we call it square."

"I'll decide when I get the package whether we're square."

Saturday morning, while I waited in the car several doors down, Kirsten's bare legs and white flip-flops flip-flopped her to the iron fence. She stood by the gate staring at the statue. Her jean shorts and red tank top definitely gave the property a touch of energized life. But what gave me a jolt as I watched her return to the car was a familiar natural grace in the movement of her body that returned my mind to whoever it was I remembered walking this way, with the natural rhythm of a ballet dancer. Parsons, the detail guy, would say that everyone has their own inherited walking style. I had never thought seriously about inherited walking styles, until now.

She came up to the car window and leaned in close. "There's a path from the back fence of the property to the statue. One board is missing. Someone from that house, directly behind the Lazore on the next street over, is coming here to visit the statue."

I got out of the car and followed her to the iron fence. Sure enough, a path led to a house on Howland. I said, "Probably a shortcut for kids going to school. No one is looking after the grounds so no one cares."

I followed her along the iron fence to the far corner of the property.

She said, "The statue makes it look like an overgrown cemetery. And the house from this angle looks like it's out of those Halloween movies, on a dead-end gravel road through the woods."

She continued to stare at the Lazore. She seemed to be reading it the way she read her Tarot cards.

"I want you to see the family pictures," I said. She gave me a sarcastic smile. "That'll cost you extra, dude, and you got to pay me in real money."

"I'll buy you lunch."

"Lunch would be great." She checked her watch. "But my shift starts at twelve."

"You're going to work dressed like that?"

"No choice, dude. If I got to pay you rent, I got to get the tips."

She returned to the car, me following.

Back in the car, she said, "How much are associate detectives making these days?"

I started the car. "That is not how you apply for a job. You explain how you will be a valuable employee and don't even talk about the pay. You tell the prospective employer — that would be me — about yourself — that would be you — like your age, previous employment, how far you went in school, and why you peek out the front window every so often."

This part of the question slipped out unintended. But there it was.

"Why does anyone peek out the window? To check the weather. The rest is none of your business."

I dropped her off at the Deuce, a low-class dive no father would allow his daughter to work at. I waited while she walked past the parked cars of the side lot and disappeared into a side entrance. For a brief second, I had that same déjà vu moment, the feeling that I had seen this person zig-zag through parking lot cars before, a uniquely fluid walking style, naturally and unintentionally graceful, a natural genetic endowment, no pretense, just how she was put together. No explanation for it.

For some reason, just then, I remembered a bust that me and Parsons had made at a strip bar. We had been sitting in the parking lot with the windows of the unmarked open; we were both chain-smokers.

Parsons had said, "The cigarettes are wrecking our lungs."

I said, "That's why we got lungs: to smoke cigarettes."

One of the strippers came out, her bikini outfit covered with a biker jacket. Her six-inch spikes wobbled her across the asphalt to my window. She said, "Hi Quinn. Remember Carmen? She's pregnant."

As a police officer, I wasn't allowed to get involved. But Carmen did not belong in a strip club. From talking to her, just passing conversation, we had coffee a couple of times, I had concluded she was there because it was the only way she knew how to get male attention. The more she got, the more she wanted and the deeper she went, like being thirsty when you're drowning. At least that would explain the stripper part. From other things she said it seemed like, from abusive fathering, she felt shameful and empty, so to fill her emptiness, she did what was shameful. That was the second part. But I'm no shrink. These daddy-issues conclusions I put together from conversations. Who knows what makes people do what they do.

Not that long ago, I'd have said watching Kirsten disappear into this sleazy bar: It happens, that's life, that's how it works. That's how the cookie crumbles, go home with a six-pack and watch the football. But this attitude had changed, like my mind had divided itself into Before Kirsten and After Kirsten. I thought: Here I am, sitting in the parking lot having just delivered this girl to the Double Deuce Tavern, which could just as easily be a strip club, which is where she's going to end up. Unless I intervene.

Or maybe it was Before Mario's Baby and After Mario's Baby. One mistake and one more little girl ends up in the mud.

Chapter Five

Nine o'clock Wednesday morning, while I was having my Tim Hortons double-double in my Dupont Street office, I received a call from a woman who introduced herself as Lorna Banks. She lived on Howland, the street next to Brunswick. I finished my coffee and locked the front door. I slowed on the way by the Lazore to sneak a look into the backyard. A search of historic properties had indicated that the Lazore was designated heritage because of its high ceilings, twelve-inch baseboards, ornate molding, double chimney, and hurricane doors.

With time to kill before my ten o'clock with this Lorna Banks, I parked in front of the Lazore. I waded through the weeds of the side yard to the back. There was no indication of anyone using the space, or the rest of the property, except a bare spot by the back door which hooked into the path Kirsten had noticed. Next to it was the outside basement entrance with the folding up "hurricane doors." I had heard of the "hurricane entrance" in old houses but had never seen one.

I returned to my car, made a right on Bloor, another right on Howland, and stopped at 233, the address Lorna Banks had given. From the sidewalk, I saw that the path from the Lazore ended in the yard of 220 Howland, the house directly across from the Banks's residence.

A ring of the bell at 233 Howland was answered by a thin woman with longish black hair under a Tilley hat. She was dressed in slacks and a sweatshirt and carried gardening gloves in one hand. Her face was beginning to line, so I guessed early forties.

"I belong to our Safe Neighbourhood group," said Mrs. Banks. "Rachelle Collins of the Shepherd Foundation gave me your number."

Her handshake was weak and clammy. Mrs. Banks did not waste time with pleasantries, like inviting me in. "According to almost everyone, the Lazore is haunted."

"I don't think there's any such thing. But it certainly looks haunted. The thing is, the Lazore was investigated after each of those little girls disappeared and nothing turned up. It was the same then as now. Deserted. No one living there. I don't know the particulars; I wasn't on the case. But after all the evidence was sorted through, and the nanny was charged, found guilty, and put away, there was nothing more to be done. I don't want to waste anyone's money, but I'm certain you will find someone who will."

"But the most important evidence, the bodies, were never recovered."

"They searched the yard with ground-penetrating radar, Mrs. Banks."

She looked doubtful. "Ground-penetrating radar is far from accurate, Mr. Quinn. I'm sure you know that. Why don't I find out if my group, along with the Shepherd group, can give you a small retainer? You spend a few days on it, and you keep the money no matter what you decide."

"The answer is the same."

"What if I remind you each of the girls disappeared in June? And what if I tell you that this is June? And that a little girl has just moved into 222 Howland? And that we're worried that it's going to happen again, soon?"

One, two, three. Next comes four, that's how serial murders work. "What do you know about the house across the street, 220 Howland?"

She glanced over my shoulder at the property. "Lois Miller, an elderly lady. She goes to my church. She takes in sewing. Lives alone. But she is peculiar."

"In what way?"

She hesitated. "Step inside, Mr. Quinn." She led him to the living room window. "She's got those flowers pinned to the front door."

I squinted them into focus. "Is it some sort of bouquet?"

"But she doesn't garden, doesn't do anything to her yard. A man comes once in a while and cuts the weeds along the front with a lawnmower, but that's it."

I shrugged. "I don't see why that's strange."

"I didn't either, until the minister, Reverend Beachy, asked me, 'Have you noticed anything strange about Lois?' This got me thinking, so I went up to her door. That thing is an occult symbol."

"Nothing illegal about that."

Mrs. Banks turned to face me. "Do you have any children, Mr. Quinn?"

"I don't, no."

She hesitated. "You don't know or you don't?"

"I don't. I can't. A football injury in high school."

She blushed. "Oh, well. None of my business."

"Not at all. Spinal cord nerve damage, one of those things. Life happens."

She continued. "My little girl, Linda, was six years old. She was the first to disappear." Her lips tightened as she struggled to control her tears. "Life happens and then life ends. But not with a child."

She reached out and took my hand. "I have never stopped looking. The imitation flower on the door, for example, there's some kind of unusual cross symbol in the middle. Lois wears the same cross symbol around her neck, like a crucifix but not a crucifix. You see, when a child goes missing, every minor detail becomes a significant event: a stranger on the street, a late-night phone call, and yes, a peculiar symbol on a door. But it's that old house that keeps all of us awake at night. You see, we're convinced our little girls are buried somewhere on the Lazore property."

"In other words, Mrs. Banks, it's *you* who is haunted, not the Lazore."

"Haunted, yes. The death of a child is like a stone dropped in still water. The concentric circles of despair never stop spreading out."

My memory flashed back to that baby dropping like a stone into rushing water as Mrs. Banks's words like concentric circles repeated themselves in my mind. From my car I phoned Kirsten. "I'll take you for early lunch and then drive you to work if you take a quick look around the house backing onto the Lazore property. Give the joint a reading, check out a weird cross symbol. I'll pick you up in twenty minutes."

Kirsten was sitting in what had become *her* chesterfield, eating gummy bears and reading her horoscope. She was dressed the part, a blue medallion of some sort around her neck, dangly earrings, black sweater, braided rope bands around each wrist, and distressed jeans with the knees poking out.

We drove three blocks along Bloor Street and parked.

"This is where you take me to lunch? Tim Hortons?"

"An early lunch, different from a lunch-time lunch. I don't want you to blame me for you being late for work."

She did some exaggerated eye-rolling I thought anatomically impossible, but she climbed out of the car and followed me to the counter where she ordered a coffee and a donut.

"You call that lunch?"

"No, I do not. If you invite me for lunch, you're going to have to do better than Tim Hortons."

I ordered coffee and an egg salad sandwich. We carried our trays to the one empty seat next to a gathering of old ladies.

"Lunch at Tim Hortons. I can't believe it."

"Beneath the status of a barmaid?"

"Not beneath the status of a detective, obviously. Did you know the greatest crimes in the world are created by the people who pretend to be following the rules, such as police officers and detectives?"

"Meaning?"

"The rule is, if the detective invites the young lady to lunch, he follows the rules and takes her to a real restaurant lunch."

I finished my egg salad and sat back to watch Kirsten with her donut. She was holding it with the thumb and forefinger of her left hand, breaking off small pieces with her right. I had not seen anyone eat a donut that way but now, watching her, it seemed familiar, a minor observation that gave me not a nudge nor a poke but a push backward in time to ... what? I did not know. Blank. This was what it must feel like to have Alzheimer's, I thought. Jesus, I'm only forty-three.

"Dude, why are you staring at me?"

"I can walk into a restaurant and peg a person's social class and family background simply by watching them eat."

"None of your business how I eat."

"The donut. You eat daintily, the same way you drink your weird tea. Someone somewhere along the Kirsten heritage line has taught her manners."

The thing was, ever since Kirsten had moved in, questions about her background had been tugging at the back of my mind like a child at a father's pant leg. Maybe she had an absent father and, when she arrived at my door, her brain said: "father figure." This might be related to the peeking out the window; I was providing a paternal protection function against whoever it was she was afraid of.

"Tell me about yourself, Kirsten."

"I'm not here to tell you about myself. I'm here because I was promised a free lunch. Next time, do your own investigating. What do you need me for anyway?"

"That blue thing hanging from your neck almost into your coffee. What is that?"

She held it up. "It's a karma stone. It contains the memory of the sky. The sky sees everything and remembers everything."

"Explain to me what karma means. How does it work?"

She gave it some thought, her eyes looking off. "The sky is your witness, like an overhead mirror staring back at you, registering all that you do and all that you don't do and all that you should do. There is the Cosmic Conscience, called 'IT,' and there is the individual conscience called 'I.' I am part of IT and IT is part of I."

"Like Jesus is watching us."

"Jesus is a metaphor for the relationship between I and IT. We are endless circles with centres everywhere, their circumferences nowhere."

I was about to reply with a "Huh?" when I remembered the time I should have arrested Carmen, the stripper, for marijuana possession. I remembered feeling that the cloudy sky was looking down at me, watching me walk her across the parking lot. I remembered that as I hesitated at the door of the unmarked trying to decide, the sun broke out from behind a cloud and the clear blue sky looked down on us and I saw that Carmen had eyes as blue as that sky. I didn't book her. I drove her home. My conscience felt good about it, which I now supposed was like my *I* feeling good about *IT*.

"So now the barmaid is a theologian. Good. Okay. That is why I brought you into this official Quinn and Associates investigation. Ask IT what it knows about the cross symbol on the door of 220. The woman's name is Lois Miller. Her back fence is the one with the board missing that opens to the path you noticed leading to the statue."

Kirsten sat quietly eating, thinking her thoughts. She said, "I have to see it."

We parked a few doors down from 220 Howland, got out, and strolled past the house.

Kirsten said, "The bartender at the Deuce told me one of his customers walks his dog on Brunswick. It refuses to walk in front of the Lazore. It has to cross the street."

"Meaning?"

"Your horoscope says, 'This is a good month to follow hunches.'"

"What's the hunch?"

"That's why we're here, big boy. You had a hunch about a weird cross. That's why you called me and promised me lunch if I investigated your hunch, which you still owe me for, by the way."

"Big boy?"

"How tall are you, dude?"

"Six foot four, two-twenty, the same now as I was twenty years ago."

"Did you wear big-boy jeans when you were a little boy?"

I had never been good at flippant conversations, especially not with a smart-ass woman. But this time I had a comeback. "Did you know your jeans are ripped?"

She looked down at herself. "You're going to say I should get my money back."

"What happened to the acid-wash style?"

"That's like eighties, dude, post-hippie."

We were standing in front of 220.

I said, "The cross symbol with the flowers is on the front door. She must change them every day: they're fresh."

Kirsten stepped closer. "How did you ever get to be a detective? The flowers are plastic."

I took out my pad and sketched the shape of the cross. She moved closer. She nudged my arm. She whispered, "Listen."

I listened.

Kirsten said, "I can hear the whirr of some kind of machine coming from inside. Stopping and starting again. A sewing machine, it sounds like. Definitely getting some hunches from that. Take me around to the front of the Lazore."

We returned to the car, made two rights, and stopped. We got out and walked to the corner of the Lazore property. The late morning sun was slanting on the base of the statue, which, I noted, was swarming with flies. I pointed, "What does that mean?"

"Don't know. Show me what you drew."

I showed her the sketch.

"I'm not up on symbols, but that upside-down crucifix is a curse sign and the flower arrangement is a passion symbol ... and there's a well-worn path leading from the back fence to the statue of Gabriella, who is looking at us now with a reproachful stare."

"Reproachful?"

"Cautionary."

"Statues can't see."

"It's not what they see, dude. It's what you see in them."

"What do you see?"

"I see that the statue is in the shade. It should have moss on it. It's being taken care of by somebody. Hence, therefore, ergo, the path." Kirsten checked her watch. "That is my reading."

"That's it? I bought you Tim Hortons and that's all I get? No wonder you're thinking reproachful."

"If you want a written report, here it is. You invoke the devil by holding a crucifix upside down and saying the Lord's Prayer backward. Write that in your pretend detective notepad. You don't even have a gun. If you want more information, I want a real lunch with a real detective. Okay, forget the gun. Somewhere upscale. That's why women cheat on their husbands. Husbands are Tim Hortons; wives are Chez Paris. I hear it all the time. Another double shot, cry me a river."

I said, "I see it all the time. The woman draws some poor bugger into a no-return minefield of cheating because she wants better than Tim Hortons."

She sighed. "Yeh, dude. You should give out your cards at the Deuce. There's a Tim Hortons on every corner and in every one of those is a husband being cheated on. Time to take me to work, big boy."

We returned to my car. I said, "Usually when I was driving with my ex, I would slide in my Waylon Jennings CD so I wouldn't have to listen to her non-stop blather about Tim Hortons."

I slipped in my Waylon Jennings and waited. When she didn't have anything smart ass to say, I said, "I'm turning on my Waylon Jennings."

I waited. I said, "My ex called him Wailing Jenny."

"Your ex again. Are you still in love with her? Don't answer. Who can understand the madness that drives people to get married in the first place, not me that's for sure. No wonder there's a Tim Hortons on every corner. That's three I've counted just in the space of you blabbering about Waylon Jennings. I'm late for work. I'm surprised the way you drive we've gotten this far. You drive like an old woman, Tim Hortons double-double, Wailing Jenny, moan-moan about the ex... I don't blame her for divorcing you."

As I pulled up to the Deuce, I glanced along the street and into the parking lot, but there were no motorcycles. She got out and said, "See ya." I watched her walk to the entrance. Today she looked like a high school kid on her way for a Big Mac. I imagined the pleasure I would get ejecting the biker that laid a hand on her through the front door. Then I thought, Why am I having these feelings? They're no different from the jealous insanity of my clients. Jealous? No. Possessive might be a better word. No. Protective, yes. I didn't want to see her end up in a biker strip joint.

I thought, I should go into the Deuce, see what the place looks like, see what her sleazy boss looks like. But no, I had promised myself I wouldn't get involved with her problems. I had also said I wouldn't get involved in the case of the missing girls. But I had to admit, now that I had already started to investigate the Lazore with Kirsten, my otherwise boring life was getting kind of interesting.

Chapter Six

I googled 220 Howland and learned that a Lois Miller owned the property. The sewing-machine sound Kirsten had heard led me to a "seamstress" search in the Brunswick Avenue area. This resulted in Lois's Alterations, 220 Howland. I had nothing that needed mending or fixing, but Kirsten probably did, so when she returned from work, I asked her. She disappeared upstairs and came back with a blue top that had lightning bolts down one shoulder in some kind of astrological pattern of planets.

She must have read my look. "Zodiac signs, dude. This one is Sagittarius and this one Cancer and this one is Mars and this one that other one; and it's missing three buttons."

"Whatever it's missing, it's not worth the cost to fix it. It'll look suspicious."

Ten minutes later when she returned in a blue evening gown and heels, her hair somehow tousled into a fashionable pile, I thought, Wow! It would have taken my ex an entire week of hairdos and fittings, not to mention credit card statements, to put this outfit together.

"Perfect," I said. "But what needs altering?"

"The hem needs raising. Two inches."

My look of disapproval sent her back upstairs.

I settled myself into the chesterfield to wait for my eyes to be filled with her next example of fashion-show brilliance not in need of alteration. Young women were magical like that, able to look like teenagers one minute and mature women the next, whereas boys could only look the age they were.

She returned carrying the dress and wearing a conservative sleeveless blouse and white capris arrangement. "This is the only other dress I've got. All my clothes come from a second-hand thrift shop on Bloor next to the pawnshop and none of them are dresses."

My *tap-tap* on the door of 220 was answered by a tall, thin woman wearing dark slacks and a white top.

"It's a bit late," I apologized. "Oh my goodness, eight o'clock. We can come back another time."

Without giving the woman time to answer, Kirsten said, "It's probably not worth the alteration fee but this was a gift from my mother."

Kirsten handed Lois the dress.

"My mother never seems to remember anything she gives me but the minute I throw something away she'll ask where is it. So he said," she gestured at me, "you better get it fixed or she'll be upset."

That she presented me as her maybe father delighted me; I felt so pleased that she would see me that way that I almost forgot why I was there. But while Kirsten and Lois were in the kitchen doing the pinning, I did manage to snoop. Nothing but old furniture and dreary wallpaper in a musty atmosphere, typical of an elderly woman living alone. Not typical was the fact that there were no family pictures, no knick-knacks, no books other than a Bible on the end table by the easy chair. I had picked it up, thinking there might be an underlined reference to the cross symbol, when I noticed, tucked in at the back, the St. John's Presbyterian Church Newsletter featuring the pastor, Reverend Raymond Beachy.

Kirsten appeared, Lois behind her.

Lois asked, "What are you looking for?"

"This is the King James version," I said. "I like it better than the new ones."

Lois looked around, as though she was checking for something missing. The fingers of her left hand were fidgeting with the thimble on her right index finger. If she'd been a smoker, now would be the time she would light up.

Kirsten jumped in. "We're Baptist, so we have a red Bible. My mother is Catholic. She has a black Bible."

Smart as a whip this barmaid, now going through her purse pretending to look for money. "Lois needs thirty dollars cash. She works with cash, no receipt, pay in advance."

I gave her a twenty and a ten. At the door, I said, "I think there's a Presbyterian church not far from here."

Lois said, "St John's, yes."

"The pastor is Reverend Beachy, I think. Have you always lived in this area?"

"I'm from Montreal originally."

"The cross on the door is Catholic," said Kirsten. "Why did you switch to Presbyterian?" Lois was fidgeting with the thimble, taking it off, putting it on. "I was raised a Catholic. I like the symbol."

"The suffering?"

"I suppose."

"We Baptists," I said, "we don't usually have symbols. But lots of suffering."

"Come back in a week. It'll be ready." Lois eased the door shut, anxious to end the conversation, it felt like, and send us on our way.

"Are you really a Baptist?" asked Kirsten in the car.

"I am now."

"A seamstress with a sewing machine in the kitchen but no sewing room. And you saw how nervous she was."

I made a right onto Bloor Street. "And I saw no pictures on the walls."

Kirsten said, "That's because her pictures are hanging on the walls of the Lazore. Her kitchen window looks directly across to the Lazore backyard. A window in the Lazore looks directly across into Lois's kitchen window. Her window has no curtain or blind. Someone with binoculars could stand in the Lazore and watch Lois in her kitchen. Someone in Lois's kitchen could stand at the window and watch Gabriella in the Lazore kitchen."

"Gabriella is dead."

"You just got finished talking to Gabriella. If I were you, I would be saying to the Shepherd Foundation, 'Where do I sign?'"

"I've just talked to Lois. I'm not convinced there's anything in need of detecting and therefore anything in need of signing."

"Get off the fence, dude. The three mothers need closure. For them closure won't happen until the thought of their missing child stops waking them up in the dead of night. Dead of night, dude. Get it? It's like a wound that can't be healed. It's like a spoon in the heart that endlessly stirs. Besides, you need the money."

"I get it, Kirsten. But the reason I retired was to get away from tragedies like drowned babies and murdered children. I can't do the dead of night stuff anymore."

She looked at me, maybe understanding my reluctance. I wasn't sure, but that was her look.

Back home, while Kirsten, now dressed in her bathrobe and PJs and slippers, watched the Ducks, I settled down at my computer in my make-shift office. The desk was small, so my printer was sitting on the bed. I had planned to move it to make room for a larger desk and a shredder but hadn't got around to it yet, now that so much of my free time was spent with Kirsten.

I googled Dr. Lazore and, after some wandering, I ended up researching the history of mental health treatment in Toronto. I was surprised to find a detailed write-up on the doctor, posthumously honoured in 2019 at a mental health convention. The article mentioned the statue of his daughter Gabriella, born June 3, 1943, erected in his honour. This made no sense. The statue was supposed to be in the doctor's honour. There was no indication of when Gabriella died, so it was possible she was still alive. Somewhere.

I said to Kirsten, who had left the Ducks during the commercials and was looking over my shoulder, "It says the statue was carved in 1988 by Arnold Lenssen, who was commissioned by the lawyer who probated the Lazore will."

I googled Arnold Lenssen, who was easy to find, still in business at Lenssen Stone Masons.

Kirsten said, "Let's pay him a visit. I'm your daughter and I think we need brickwork done on our house. It's called pointing."

So now from a tenant who doesn't pay rent to a tenant who acts like it's her house. I would have been enjoying the fantasy more had there not been so many questions that I knew would not leave me alone until I got answers. "Kirsten, could we have a little talk?"

She stepped back, looking big-eyed innocent like a child about to be scolded for she didn't know what. She sat on the bed.

Her looking at me like that made me wonder what I was going to talk about. Her moving uninvited into my space, referring to me as her father, paying no rent, peeking out the window, working her way into my detective agency and then, with all those questions that needed answers, pretending she had no idea what we needed to talk about?

"How old are you, Kirsten, if you don't mind me asking."

"I do mind you asking."

"I'd say twenty-five."

"Why do you want to know?"

"I should have had a rental agreement for you to give me background info, previous addresses, and so on. I don't even know your last name."

"Who, what, where, why? You're the detective."

"There are nicer apartments all over the city. Why did you choose mine? It doesn't even have a stove."

"Who, what, where, why? You're the detective."

"Why is it every time I ask a question you come back with a smart-ass high-school-kid attitude?"

She folded one leg over the other. She said, "Let's consider Mrs. Ex. I was snooping through your stuff and I found some pictures. She doesn't look that bad. She could lose a few pounds, she could do something with her hair, have her teeth whitened, some wrinkle cream would help, a nose job would make her eyes look bigger, implants would help, otherwise, not bad. So what happened with you and Mrs. Ex?"

"She currently lives with an electrician, and you're not supposed to snoop through my stuff. And it's none of your business what happened with Mrs. Ex."

"There's my answer. None of your business."

I turned off the laptop and we went into the living room to sit on the chesterfield to wait for episode six of the Ducks, a program beneath even my intelligence. Yet, here I was watching it.

At commercials, she said, "If you make me a partner in your detective business, I'll tell you everything about me. The first item of business, how much are you going to pay?"

"Thirty per cent."

"Of what?"

"Nothing. I have no new contracts, except maybe the Shepherd."

"So take the Shephard and give me thirty per cent."

She kicked off her slippers and turned toward me sideways, one leg folded up, her bare foot rocking time with the other folded down. It was another familiar gesture catching my attention unexpectedly. She said, "However, before I agree to your offer, excuse me very much, but maybe if you dressed a little better you might be doing a little better? Like you've only got three suits in your closet and your ties aren't in style and your car is a piece of junk and your office on Dupont is a hole in the wall. I went down and had a look. If you want to be prosperous, you have to look prosperous. If you want to run with the big dogs you have to bark like the big dogs. Quinn and Associates, one hundred and twenty offices worldwide plus a member of Interpol. Stuff like that. And this apartment you're renting me, you advertised it as furnished. You think I should pay rent for an apartment with no pictures, no potted plants, no knick-knacks, and furniture that sucks. Down here is bad enough. Upstairs is worse."

"So move."

"I like your TV."

Kirsten picked up the remote and turned up the volume and the Ducks returned and I stared at the bare walls of my apartment. She was right. It could use a little spruce up. I said, "Maybe you could help me. A coat of paint. New curtains."

When she said "Okay," what happened to me was like magic. For the first time in months, I wanted to spruce up my living quarters. She would help with the colour scheme. We would go shopping for decent furniture. I felt the urge to give her a fatherly hug as I settled back to watch Jase Duck getting his first hair cut. Jase liked the hairdresser, enjoyed the girl's conversation, felt like a new man, until, in addition to the upfront fee, the girl wanted a tip. He refused and the girl put on a fake show of tears and a long story about overdue rent, so he gave in.

The warning bells of manipulation had sounded, as they should have the day Kirsten arrived, but like Jase Duck, I was enjoying her conversation and felt like a new man.

Chapter Seven

Emily and Ramona were sitting on the chesterfield watching *Survivor* and eating fig bars. Ramona said, "The stuff in the middle looks like black driveway pavement, and that's what gives my belly the spare tire."

She patted her stomach.

"Uncle Gomez back home got his spare tire from eating nothing but instant noodles. He wore a T-shirt that said, 'real men eat instant noodles.' He wrote the company and asked if they would make fig-bar-flavoured instant noodles."

Emily waited at the back door for the ring of Lois's little bell, the signal to meet Lois at the fence. If Ramona, the babysitter, was talking on the phone or watching television, Emily would quietly open the back door and creep across the grass and wait for Lois to bring the doll. If the woman didn't appear, she would try later.

She watched as the leaves from the dead tree in the Lazore yard, chased by the wind blowing in from the street, piled themselves against the stone foundation of Lois's house. A fly landed on Emily's left arm, crawled a few steps, then flew off. It circled and came back to land on her right hand. Sometimes flies landed in a hole in the foundation of Lois's house and disappeared into a crack that was shaped like an S. Sometimes they flew up into patches of sunlight in the grass by the statue that liked to scare the kids walking past the Lazore on their way home from school.

Lois's head popped up from the other side of the fence. "Do you want to see the doll?"

Emily tugged at the hem of her skirt. She looked back to make certain Ramona was inside. Emily touched the doll's tiny hand and ran one finger along the curve of the smiley face. She felt the wool hair, which was almost the same colour as hers.

"See, Emily? I've made a little red skirt like the one you wear and I'm going to sew little white knee socks like you wear. I'm going to call the doll Isabela."

"Oh," said Emily. She was not surprised. All the dolls Lois brought to the fence were called Isabela.

"Do you see who she looks like?"

"Me."

"But her name is not Emily. It's Isabela."

"Can I hold her?"

"Of course."

"Can I keep her?"

"She's got to stay with her big sister in the basement."

"Maybe she needs a hat."

"She doesn't need a hat in the basement. But you can rock her if you want so she doesn't start to cry."

Emily held the doll against her chest, stroking its soft wool hair. She curled herself around it to keep it out of the wind and rocked it gently.

"I better take her inside before she starts to cry," said Lois.

"Why will she cry?"

"Babies get colic sometimes."

"Where is her big sister?"

"I keep her in the basement out of the wind so she doesn't catch a cold and get colic. Would you like to meet her someday?"

Emily nodded.

"Don't tell your babysitter or your mother. The doll and the sister are a secret."

"Well, well," said Ramona, hoisting Emily onto the chair with the booster seat. "Ready for lunch?"

"Why is it always ham sandwiches?"

"Where I come from, we eat ham sandwiches every day for lunch."

"And Jell-O?"

"Yes, and Jell-O."

While they were eating the Jell-O, Emily asked, "How many days is it until my birthday, Ramona?"

"Birthday! June 15. Only one more week."

"Remember, I want a doll's house."

"A little red one, yes. Who were you talking to at the fence?"

"No one."

"And what did no one want?"

"To say hello."

"That's nice. In Colombia, everyone is friendly. Not here, except for dogs. Everyone is friendly to dogs here, sleep with them even."

"Can we read the dog story at nap time and do some printing?"

"In Colombia, I never went to school but I learned to speak good English from my uncle who does business over here. Now I am learning to read along with you. My daughter wants to come to Canada as a nanny but I tell her we don't make much money and work long hours so some nannies must find other ways to make money, so they work for my uncle. His job is to arrange surprise trips to Disneyland."

Emily poked at her Jell-O, watching it jiggle. "My mother eats Jell-O to lose weight."

"Powder, that's all it is. It says on the package 'just add two cups of water.' My uncle asks me, how do you get two cups of water into one little package?"

Emily scooped up a spoonful, tilted her head, and dropped the Jell-O into her mouth.

"Would you like to go to Disneyland, Emily?"

Emily nodded.

"My uncle sells the vacation package, one week of magical fun. Would you like to see some pictures?"

Emily nodded. Ramona hurried away. She returned in a few moments with a picture album of Disneyland Adventures. While Ramona tidied away the dishes, Emily looked through the pictures of Big Thunder Mountain Railroad.

Chapter Eight

Today, Kirsten was wearing the blue medallion and the big ring earrings and numerous wrist bracelets. Her hair was combed sideways and she was wearing a ripped jean jacket, tight black sweater, jean skirt, and ripped leggings. The twelve-inch heels, well, six-inch, one fastened with a green leather strap, and the other with red, elevated her to almost my height. Just when I thought I had adjusted to her crazy get-ups, she appeared in one even crazier.

The stretches between lights on Davenport were moving well, I thought, until Kirsten said, "This is like driving Aunt Bessie. She would sit in the backseat ramrod straight and say, 'Turn here, park there.' Why are you driving so slow?"

Despite the six-inch heels, she had managed to fit herself into a horizontal slouch so she could do her sullen teenager act, tapping her red fingernails on the sky pendulum thing.

I said, "I used to smoke. Mrs. Ex would sit in the backseat and crank down the window of my old Kia and say, 'Smoking in a car should be illegal and you should be arrested.'"

"At this rate, it'll take us six days to get to Lenssen Stone Masons."

"It took Mrs. Ex six months before she was telling me how to drive, sitting ramrod straight where you're sitting now in a slouch, until she moved into the backseat like Aunt Bessie."

"So, what happened?"

"With what?"

"You and Mrs. Ex?"

"If I tell you my history, will you tell me yours?"

"Try me."

"She was an Anglican, worked long hours at the church, labouring for the refugees. She tabulated and calculated the food bank donations. Washed and folded the donated clothing, worked with landlords for cheap housing."

"Cry me a river."

"And slept with the priest."

Sigh, pout, eye-rolling. "Bummer."

I picked up speed.

"How did you find out? Hire a detective?"

"I had some clothes to donate. So, I went to church. I couldn't find her so I went to the priest's apartment in the church. I would have left the clothes but the door was unlocked. I noticed a bible on the dining room table with a note sticking out. I'm a snoop by nature, same as you, so I read the note she'd written to the priest."

"Double bummer..."

"The priest apologized for the error in his ways, gave up being a priest, and became an electrician."

"That's it? And you got divorced and she got all your money?"

I noted her question. "What money are you thinking about?"

"Well, I don't know. Half of whatever you've got."

"Parsons thought I should go after the church for alienation of affection by a person in authority and be duly compensated, but I couldn't be bothered. So, I decided to take in a rent-paying tenant to help cover expenses."

This hint didn't seem to bother her. Teenage entitlement apparently lasted well into the thirties. It was like living for free in a parent's basement, except in this case, she was living for free upstairs.

She pulled herself up off her spine. "I listen to tragic-story-time every day at the bar and each story causes me to reflect." She held out her blue-sky thing. "The fact is, no matter how much reflecting one does, the wheel of fortune takes one where it wants one to go. It's called destiny."

My reflecting on my destiny had never included a freeloader appearing in my life. And I was questioning the no-tips story. Either she was getting them and not telling me, or the Double Deuce's male customers were not being driven by their inner pig-dog instincts, which was unlikely. And now the fact that she had brought up Mrs. Ex and my money bothered me. Otherwise, I would not have said, "You're too young to understand anything about life taking anybody anywhere. You think you just bop around, go where you please, crash for free here and there, make voodoo tea without having to buy your own voodoo bags, half the time not even bothering to throw them in the garbage. But, eventually, life catches up with you."

That sarcasm should have made her feel guilty. Instead, she said, "Excuse me very much, dude, but what in the world are you talking about with your pompous superior attitude? Thanks for not giving me the bouquet-flavoured BS edition I would expect from someone your age. But what we're really talking about is karma. You get what you deserve. You got cheated on because you deserved to get cheated on. You're a Tim Hortons guy."

So, another clever trick, flip the blame. Blame for what?

Arnie Lenssen looked like a Tim Hortons guy: a stocky man in his fifties with a thick-fingered handshake, palms as hard as brick. Arnie gave her a Tim-Hortons-guy appraisal. I could see that Kirsten's side-saddle braid and the tight sweater and the jean skirt were driving his cement-mixer thoughts down a very curvy road.

I thought, Get ready, Arnie, for she will use these curves, one after another, to trick you into getting what she wants. I watched her do it. She was like a puppeteer. She extended her handshake just long enough to get him on her string. After that, every look she gave him got her a double look back. For every move she made, she doubled her investment.

"I do mostly tuckpointing and bricklaying," Lenssen was telling her, ignoring me. "I'll take your address and drive over for a look and write you an estimate."

"My father," she gestured in my direction, "isn't much of a handyman. Useless, in fact. We might have other repairs you might be interested in looking at."

Lenssen glanced at the useless me. "Pointing takes skill, otherwise you make a mess. And yes, I can do other things."

"He's useless in the kitchen too, but he can definitely make a mess."

Lenssen scowled at me, waiting, it seemed, for me to defend myself.

"I understand you carved the Lazore statue." Kirsten was moving him into the con.

"Oh, that. I did the pointing on the Lazore house when it was in probate. The deal was, give me the contract and I'll do the statue. Back then I did some carving in concrete. I gave it up because there was no demand. The lawyer didn't care what the statue looked like long as it was a statue, like the will said, to be placed on an eight-by-eight concrete slab eight inches thick in the exact spot marked on a hand-drawn map. The lawyer, I can't remember his name, gave me a photograph of Dr. 'Gabrielle' Lazore and his daughter, Gabriella, standing side by side. He said to copy Gabriella."

"I've often wondered about that," said Kirsten. "Why not the doctor?"

Lenssen smiled. "When I had finished and put the statue where they said, the lawyer came by and said, 'You were supposed to do the doctor.' So, I showed him the work order and said if you want me to do it again, it'll cost you. Dr. Lazore's first name was spelled Gabrielle on the paper. I think he didn't want to admit he had made a mistake with the spelling of the name, so there Gabriella stands."

"Do you have the photograph?" asked Kirsten. "I'm interested in heritage buildings. The Lazore has such an interesting history."

Lenssen hesitated, but Kirsten made a move with her natural endowments so subtle that Lenssen couldn't see it working on him. He led her past a flat-bed truck into the shop, which contained three cement mixers, some shovels, hooks along one wall for levels and trowels, everything neat and organized. I followed quietly behind. She talked a blue streak of nonsense about her interest in heritage buildings, accidentally bumping his shoulder as they made their way to his battered cabinet in one corner of the shop so he could paw through the files to whatever she wanted and hand her exactly that.

"Can I borrow this picture for a day or so? I'm interested in statues, like in graveyards, but this one is unique."

"Of course. I've been hanging onto the paperwork in case someone decides to sue me for carving the wrong statue. But you can borrow the photograph."

Kirsten took the picture to a side window for a better look. "Do you know anything about Gabriella?"

"Nothing. I drive by the house from time to time to see if the statue is still okay. Funny thing. It sits in the shade so it should be covered with moss but it's perfectly clean after all these years. I got out of my car once and went to the door to ask what was being used to keep the concrete clean. I was going to offer to do it to make sure it's done right, you know, not using strong cleaners. But the place was empty. I went over and looked at the statue again. I couldn't understand it. Algae, lichen, reindeer moss all love statues."

"So, who's keeping it clean?"

"I don't know. I just know that after all these years, it's still clean."

"What does it mean," Kirsten continued, "when flies are swarming around its base?"

"Cluster flies. Botflies. Something is rotting nearby, probably a dead squirrel or a mouse or a bird. The flies lay their eggs in the carcass and the larvae live off the rotting matter."

She made a disgusted squirming pupae face but Lenssen went on.

"I took a trip to India and saw the rotting bodies in the Ganges with swarms of flies on the corpses and then the same flies on the meat hanging in the market. From there the flies moved along to the vegetables. The street vendors buy the vegetables and serve them unwashed from their carts. The carp eat the bodies in the water and the people on the shore stand there with fishing poles."

It looked as though Kirsten was going to lose her breakfast, so I stepped in. I thanked Lenssen for the photograph, said we would be in touch regarding the estimate, and we returned to the car.

"Take the photograph to Pond's, the photo place," said Kirsten. "I bet if they do a reprint, it will come out like brand new."

"I'd like to know who's cleaning the statue."

"Gabriella. If someone carved a statue of you, wouldn't you want to keep it clean? Especially bird shit. No, you probably wouldn't care. Not even the bird shit."

She had a point. Bird shit stuck like glue on the metal hood of my car, so to get it off the rough surface of the statue would take scrub-brush scrubbings.

Kirsten continued, "I wonder what's rotting close by to draw the flies? Maybe one of the missing little girls."

"Not possible. The last one was a year ago. There'd be nothing left but bones." I thought about this. "But you're right, wrapped in plastic it might still be intact. But still, the radar would have found it."

"Maybe the radar missed it. An animal digs down, like a groundhog, and rips open the plastic and the flies go down the groundhog hole. So, on our next trip we look for groundhog holes."

I didn't believe there were any groundhogs in a downtown area. But this adventure with Kirsten was giving me more fun than I'd had in years, so, for the time being, I played along with it. But I wouldn't get involved.

I dropped her off for her Saturday shift at the Deuce. I noted no bikers. I drove home to look up Pond's on my laptop. 129 locations, it said. I delivered the photo to the closest, and having nothing to do for the hour needed to do reprints, decided to drop in at the Deuce for a beer and late lunch, served to me by Kirsten who didn't get any tips.

As I parked the car, I noticed an ape-hanger Harley out front. Kirsten stood at the taps waiting for the bartender to draw her beer, which she delivered to the Harley rider seated at the back table. He was wearing a silver chain around his neck.

"Is that the one who grabbed you?" I asked when she came to my table.

"It doesn't matter. Don't cause a scene. I'm used to it."

I ordered a draft lager and leaned back to watch him, a typical biker bottom-feeder with tattoos, earrings, and beard, like a Duck on TV, but not one that I could recognize from when I worked the strip clubs, owned by bikers. Kirsten brought my draft and took my order from the lunch menu board at the back. She made a face at my choice of hamburger and fries.

"I bet Mrs. Ex never let you eat this kind of junk."

"That's why I'm eating it now."

By the time she had delivered my meal, the Ducks Dynasty biker had downed his beer and was waving for another. As she set it down, he put his arm around her waist, maybe a friendly gesture, except that Kirsten's reaction of pulling away and backing off told me she didn't like it.

I hadn't understood why women liked to dangle the hook but when they get a bite act like they aren't fishing, until Parsons explained that women want to look sexy so they'll be looked at, not so they'll be disrespected.

Kirsten took the twenty — the biker waved off the change — and she turned to the next table, where an older man ordered a Guinness.

I finished my beer and my lunch, left a generous tip that I hoped I would get back in rent, and waved to Kirsten that I was leaving. At the biker table, I leaned over to whisper in Chain's ear, "That's my daughter you're messing with."

I reached behind me and pulled up a chair. "When she was nine years old, she had a paper route. One day she came home and said, 'The man at 46, you know with the double garage, he says come with me into my garage and I'll show you something you might like.' So, the next day I delivered the paper to number 46 and I said, 'It's my daughter who delivers the papers. Come with me into your garage and I'll show you something I know you won't like.' And I handed him his paper."

I stood and slid back my chair. "Newspapers, beer. Makes no difference to me. Touch her again and I'll show you something you won't like."

I left before the biker could react, not wanting to get Kirsten fired. She still hadn't paid any rent.

The digital reprint of the photo by Pond's Photography came out perfect. Dr. Lazore, a thin man with thin hair dressed in a suit and tie and vest, looked exhausted. Beside him stood the skinny Gabriella with pig-tailed brown hair, white blouse, plaid skirt, and knee socks. Her lower lip was pouting in a sullen attitude, like the one Kirsten had given me as I left the Deuce.

I taped the photograph to my bathroom mirror, a three-way business that Kirsten spent half her time looking into. She pretended to be casual about her appearance, wearing any old thing it seemed, putting together odd blouses and jeans and boots and scarves and earrings and hairdos. But I now knew her oddball elegance was not accidental.

I stood at the mirror, playing with the photograph, reflecting it at various angles. Something about the details of Gabriella's face haunted me in the same way as the statue. I took the photograph back to Pond's and asked them to do an eight-by-ten blow-up of Gabriella by herself. That evening, Kirsten and I stood together considering the face from various angles.

Kirsten said, "The seamstress, Lois, has a bit of a pouty lower lip like Gabriella, but you don't notice it looking at her straight on. But when she was hemming my dress, I was looking down and I noticed."

I pictured Lois Miller's face, scowly with the facial lines of a mean school teacher hardened into permanent grumpiness, but I couldn't remember a pouting lower lip. Kirsten was as good a detail person as Parsons, and as good a manipulator too. Parsons could make up a net of lies that suggested to the bad guy that Parsons knew more than he did. Kirsten's skill with clever fabrications had me wondering about her the same way my clients wondered about their cheating spouses. Kirsten had worked a con on Lenssen to get what she wanted and she was working a con on me to get what she wanted. But what did she want?

I shrugged it off. She was just a kid using her good looks to play me for free rent, no different from the strippers in the bars that played old guys for their money. I'd give her another few days and then tell her she had to move on.

Kirsten interrupted my thoughts. "Block out the face and look at the eyes."

I did. They looked like eyes. Then, as I concentrated on each individually, I felt my sight drawn into them. I could not turn away, for I saw in the lifeless stare of Gabriella's eyes in the photo the same haunting expression I saw in the stone eyes of the statue. Somehow Lenssen had managed to capture that vacant gaze.

I said, "They're pale grey, like marbles."

Kirsten looked closely. "It looks like she's wearing White Demon contact lenses. Biker chicks wear them. Which reminds me. Chains said, 'Is Rambo really your dad?' So I said, 'Yeah, he's kind of protective. I'm his only kid, you know. His usual line is, 'If you can't keep your eyes off my daughter, I will remove them. You got off lucky.'"

"Good," I said. "Tell it like it is."

"That's where you're wrong. I shouldn't have said that. That biker has a lot of biker buddies. From now on, get your lunch at Tim Hortons with the old ladies."

I must have looked as though I wasn't paying attention to her warning, which I wasn't. She added, "I'm serious, dude. You don't mess with those guys."

Chapter Nine

I arrived home at seven. Kirsten had a chicken in the oven. Jesus. It smelled delicious. What a homecoming from a hard day at the office. There she was, sitting at my kitchen table, looking almost domesticated in a plaid shirt and leggings, reading a recipe book, well, the newspaper, well, her horoscope. But not eating gummy bears or watching *Duck Dynasty*.

I said, "Do me a favour. Go into the bathroom and look at the picture of Gabriella and ask her where her baby sister is."

As though this made sense, she went into the bathroom. While she was gone, I turned on the football. She came into the living room and sat beside me. The scent of her shampoo was familiar because she had used mine. "Gabriella says wait for a full moon before you start digging."

"Digging where?"

"She says to follow the flies down the groundhog hole."

She picked up the remote and switched to the Ducks.

"Kirsten, when I rented you the apartment, did you know that you were supposed to live upstairs?"

"Of course."

"So why are you downstairs cooking a chicken?"

"I don't have an oven."

"But you have a microwave."

"How can I cook a chicken in a microwave?"

She wasn't laughing at me, but it felt like it. What would Parsons make of me if he could see me now? What would any of them at 54 Division make of me if they could see me now? Spending my evenings watching *Duck Dynasty*, a show about a family of swamp people who had made a fortune creating a call that lured ducks from miles around to the exact spot the hunters waited to blow them to pieces. But this didn't change their family values of Sunday church and honesty.

Kirsten said, "Gabriella's got a funny ear."

"What does that mean?"

"You'll soon be getting a message."

"Show me this ear." Maybe she was on to something. Ears were almost as good as fingerprints, no two exactly alike. I followed her into the bathroom.

"See this part here?" Kirsten held her left finger to one of her own lobes. "See? Mine is round. Here. Feel along here. Feel this part."

I felt her ear where she was pointing. Then she guided my finger to the exact spot in the photo. "That part is rounded."

I tried to study the photos, but I was distracted by the faint smell of the skin cream my ex wore. Mrs. Ex, put it on so thick I needed goggles to stop my eyes from smarting. Kirsten had been searching through my stuff again.

"I don't get it," I said.

She traced with her finger the ear line in the photo and then she took my finger and traced it along hers. Then she turned and did her other ear, which she seemed to think was different. But I still wasn't getting it. I reached out with my right hand and turned her head to a better light, which resulted in a sideways tilting of her chin and a parting of her lips that made me want to ask, who is this person lingering and snooping and waiting for the exact moment to step forward and say, "Guess what? I've come back."

I returned to the living room and sat down.

The Ducks, looking like they all needed to be tested for early Alzheimer's, were seated side by side having an evening prayer service. For years my ex had gone to the evening prayer service every Wednesday. She had prayed to God to please fix whatever needed fixing so that we could have children. She had said it that way although she knew I was the one who needed fixing. To adoption, I said no thank you. I had seen too many damaged kids to ever risk adopting one.

Kirsten plunked herself down beside me. She said, "If Lois the seamstress has the same ear then she is Gabriella. If she is Gabriella, she's got a guilty conscience. She's doing penance by cleaning the statue. Like Lady Macbeth, washing her hands. You probably don't know who that is. You were probably in the applied stream. The Lady Macbeth story is about how a guilty conscience will drive you to crazy behaviours."

I was on the verge of asking, why are you saying this to me when you know Mario's baby is still haunting me with a guilty conscience when she said, "Join the dots. Gabriella hasn't come back to wash her hands, but she *has* come back to wash the statue, which is basically the same thing. But no, you probably aren't good at joining dots. You were in the applied stream."

"How do you know that?"

"I was looking at your yearbook. Under your picture, you say, 'They tried to teach me cheaters don't win, but I did.' You've got a thing for cheaters. You seem to think everyone is a cheater, including me, like I'm trying to cheat you on the rent."

I let this comment go because I knew Lady Macbeth's guilty conscience idea needed to be considered. "Maybe that minister from her church, Reverend Beachy, knows something about that, a guilt thing she's talked to him about, him having a direct line to the All-Knowing."

Kirsten said, "One of the Ducks said that your conscience is the proof that God exists. But not if you're a psychopath. So, psychopaths are atheists."

"So, atheists are psychopaths. I don't think so."

Conscience, guilt, penance. My eyes involuntarily slid sideways to the neck of her shirt to see if she was wearing the blue-sky medallion. She caught my glance and pulled it out. She held it up and looked at it the way you would look into a mirror. "Do you want to know what I see? I see that now, for the first time in years, Quinn is looking forward to coming home at night, especially if Kirsten has a chicken in the oven for his dinner and, oh, what else can I see? Happy days, Quinn relaxing there on the chesterfield with Kirsten watching the Ducks. I knew it, I knew it ... I didn't see that when I first arrived, but that's what I see now, and I'm never wrong. He doesn't care that I'm a freeloader not paying rent."

She was teasing me, having a good time at my expense. "Don't kid yourself. He most certainly does care that you're a freeloader not paying rent."

Kirsten rolled her eyes. "Save yourself the strife and stress of worrying about it. You'll get your rent as soon as the tips get better."

"It's not just the rent, Kirsten. It's like I'm sitting here, waiting for a timer to go off, so the oven will get opened and I'll look inside to see that what you're cooking up might not be happy days for me."

"It's not supernatural, dude. It's a chicken I got on sale at Walmart and stuck in the oven to keep it warm."

The Ducks, now hiding in a blind waiting to shoot Daffy, were talking about how to make a gay wedding cake. Kirsten listened to their line of baking nonsense and then said, "This gives me pause. The Ducks' code of family values is anti-gay because they're church people. But it's not that long ago that these Tennessee swamp dudes were marrying their fourteen-year-old nieces."

Ahhh. There's the answer. "All this time I've been wondering what this is about. I'm a middle-aged man and you, twenty years my junior, seem to have moved in with me. You think I'm your uncle."

Kirsten rolled her eyes. "Save yourself the strife and stress of worrying about being an uncle. I'm only your tenant, not your niece. I'm here to watch the Ducks. Then I'm gone."

"A tenant who doesn't pay rent."

She disappeared upstairs. I was thinking about going to the foot of the stairs to say I was kidding, take as long as you want, when she returned with an envelope: "There. Paid in full."

I counted the money. I gave it back. "Consider it payment for coming with me to talk to Reverend Beachy."

She took it with no hesitation, almost grabbed it out of my hand.

I said, "Kirsten, you make my head spin."

"I know I do. Let's have that chicken dinner, made specially by Kirsten for her Uncle Quinn."

Chapter Ten

Lois peeked out the back door of the kitchen and then locked it. She locked the front door, then came back into the kitchen.

Emily asked, "When is your granddaughter coming?"

"She's not really my granddaughter. She's Isabela. You look like Isabela."

"Who is Isabela?"

"My little sister."

"Why do you keep looking out the kitchen window?"

"You have to be careful of the ghosts across the fence. You know what happens. The ghosts are arrested and released. Back on the street to do it all over again."

"What ghosts?"

Lois opened the freezer and unwrapped a popsicle. "Half for you and half for Isabela." She sat beside Emily. "No such thing as a cure for ghosts. Chase them away and, within a few minutes, they come back again. The neighbours want to board up the Lazore doors, and board up the Lazore windows, to shut in the ghosts. But I've got everyone fooled. There is only one ghost."

"Where's your little sister?"

"But you're safe with me. That's why, when you're here, I keep the doors locked, so the ghosts can't get in. If the doorbell rings, we don't answer. I have to keep you safe."

Lois broke the popsicle in half.

"The neighbours have tried to catch the ghost in the graveyard using flashlights. But if they'd shone the light on the face of the statue, they'd have seen in its eyes that Gabriella is the ghost."

Lois began to suck on her popsicle.

"Why are you sucking on your little sister's half?"

"I never had any children. That's why I'm spoiling you. I'm building you a doll's house. Come and I'll show you."

She led the way down the stairs into the basement. "This is my laundry area, washing machine, dryer, and behind these boxes is a secret door."

Lois pointed to a framed photograph hanging on one wall. "That's Isabela, my baby sister."

She slid aside the boxes.

"What are the boxes for?"

"You're too little to understand about these boxes."

She opened the door into a room that had a bench and another sewing machine and shelves lined with rag dolls.

"Why do you have two sewing machines?"

"This one belonged to my mother. She sewed me a doll one time and my father put a battery in it to make it cry."

Emily remembered her mother sitting at her sewing machine. Her fingers were sewing with a long needle, the tip of one finger covered with a silver pusher thing. She was the one who had taught Emily to walk, not her father, who had disappeared. Her mother had held on to her fingers, one finger in each fist, and the two of them had walked back and forth across the kitchen floor. Like this, she said, and she got up and Emily took a finger in each hand and they walked back and forth across the kitchen floor — until one day she walked on her own. It was only about two steps, but her mother had laughed and clapped and was so pleased that Emily got up again and walked to the end of the kitchen. Now her mother was too busy to do anything with Emily.

"What are the dolls' names?"

"Isabela."

"Don't they have different names?"

"This one does. This one is the priest. This one is the undertaker."

"If that half is for your sister, why are you eating it?"

"My sister is eating her half." She took Emily's hand to lead her to the workbench. "Here is the doll's house. The front opens up like this, with two floors, down and up, like the Lazore."

Lois pulled a wooden box out from under the workbench. "Here is where I keep the furniture. This little chair for the living room, this big bed for the mommy and daddy's bedroom, this little bassinette for Isabela's room. Almost every little girl who comes to play with Isabela likes going through this box of furniture. And setting up the doll's house." Lois sucked on the popsicle.

"When is your sister Isabela coming?"

"You're my sister now, Isabela."

"I have to go now," said Emily.

"You remind me so much of me when I was a little girl. Next time you come, I will show you the other Isabelas."

Chapter Eleven

I felt bad for asking for the rent money when, in fact, Kirsten had it ready to give to me. Especially since I wanted her to stay, rent money or not. The odd thing was, I found myself comparing Kirsten to Kirsten. Most of the time, Kirsten gave the impression that she was self-sufficient and well able to look after herself. But the look on her face when she peeked out the window showed me she was also a lost and frightened Kirsten. Sometimes, like when she was slouched on my chesterfield, she looked like someone who had needed my help a long time ago.

And another thing: this karmic feeling of sliding back and forth between past and present was getting to me, like the year I didn't pay my taxes. I'd entirely forgotten, but every so often when something out of nowhere jogged my mind, I'd remember. Then one day Revenue Canada showed up uninvited on my doorstep to collect, with interest.

"So, dude, to what Chez Paris are you taking me?"

"If Sailor's is good enough for me and Parsons, it's good enough for the barmaid."

"Was he a good partner?"

"The best."

"But you don't hang out with him anymore."

"We sometimes meet at Sailor's."

"Sailor's doesn't sound like Chez Paris."

"The cook is a French sailor. He cooks French-sailor fashion. Chez Sailor."

She looked doubtful but she went upstairs and, in a few minutes, appeared before me with her hair falling over one eye, her dress a high-school pongee thing I'd not seen before. Added to that were spike heels and jangly bracelets around each wrist and earrings so heavy I wondered why her ears didn't sag. I pulled on my own to gauge the weight an ear might be able to carry without being torn from the head.

"Don't get smart, Uncle Dude. Better than in my nose. But I need something around my neck, right?"

The neck of the gown looked fine to me, but without waiting for an answer she disappeared upstairs and returned wearing a silver necklace that looked like two worms tangled together at the end of a fishhook. I bent closer for a better look.

"Are you in need of those tri-focal glasses with the lines that stop you squinting?" She held it up for me. "Worms on a fishhook for going to Sailor's."

She stepped back then disappeared and returned with the blue karma thing added to the worms.

"This more suitable?"

I had no idea what this get-up might be more suitable for.

"Times up," she said. "This is what I'm wearing."

The traffic across the Lakeshore was brisk but I took the inside lane thinking, What's the hurry, enjoy the drive.

Until Kirsten started. "What time is our reservation?"

"For seven."

"If you don't speed it up, we'll get a parking ticket."

I upped the speed.

"Or are you practicing for when you drive one of those battery-powered wheelchairs?"

I wasn't going to let her smart comments ruin the evening. I slipped in my favourite George Jones CD. She listened for a minute before saying, "Dude. I'm impressed. You really are Country and Western. How cool is that? My Aunt Bessie liked country. She said if you play it backward, you'll get back your wife, your pick-up, and your dog. The way you drive, you'll get your half of the house back, your ex back, and your cop job back."

I did not admit, when we finally arrived, that thanks to my too slow driving, we were ten minutes late. No matter. I could tell she was impressed. Three walls of wood panelling were decorated with nautical paraphernalia. According to the write-up under the glass cover of the wooden captain's quarters table, the underwater junk had been rescued from long-gone Great Lakes fishing vessels. I hadn't thought about it before, but now I realized that these oddball anchors and ship wheels and nets and chains would suit Kirsten's oddball brain.

"Wow," said Kirsten, glancing around. "You outdid yourself, dude. I love it."

I held the wooden seafarer chair for her. A waiter appeared with the menu written on a buried treasure map listing the more expensive choices for the captain on one side and, for the first mate, cheaper choices on the other.

She asked, "Which one am I?"

"The first mate, so you order off the cheap side."

I noticed that Kirsten was frowning at the waiter. She seemed to be having trouble fitting him into her idea of a sailor. Sailors were rugged and tanned with big muscles. Like myself, for example. This waiter was thin and delicate.

She waited for the waiter to move out of earshot. "The Ducks would say, 'That waiter is gay as a daisy.'" She picked up the menu, glanced through it, and said, "Karma has its own menu. You get served what you deserve. So, you'll have to order for me, Captain. What do you think I deserve?"

I picked from the wine list and placed the order. The waiter gave us the eye, no doubt thinking I was an older man with an escort. This thought startled me, another one of these karmic jolts coming at me from nowhere, as so many of my thoughts were doing, arriving at random in my mind ever since Kirsten had arrived at random on my doorstep. She didn't look like an escort. At least, not now that I'd gotten used to her. She looked like Kirsten.

I asked her, "Where do random thoughts come from?"

"Where do any thoughts come from? From buried experiences stored in your subconscious. Like an IV drip running from a saline bag, our subconscious is filled with the salt of our childhood experiences. They travel the drip line into our conscious mind and then return to the bag. As long as you're stuck in the circle of your IV drip, you don't choose your thoughts; your thoughts choose you."

I was still trying to process this idea when she said, "The question is, which is stronger, the conscious mind or the subconscious? I used to imagine myself having a daughter and I would imagine treating her like my mother treated me. Just thinking about it filled me with so much rage that my heart raced and the adrenaline pumped these childhood memories through my veins from my subconscious mind to my thinking mind and back again so fast it made me dizzy."

"What did she do to you?"

"That was the problem. I wasn't sure. Well, yes. I know. She killed me. Well, she killed the child I could have been, which means she killed the adult I might have become."

She took a deep breath, like she was ready to make the confession that I had been waiting for. I sat forward, facing her, waiting. She was staring off across the water, her mind a long way off, by the look of it.

She said, "It's like if your arm gets broken, the doctor will fix it and it will heal in no time, but when the mind gets broken, the doctor can't fix that. A broken body is programmed to heal itself. We only provide a little help. A broken mind seems programmed to destroy itself. Anxieties, addictions, neuroses, and suicides. That's what my mother was about."

"She's all better now?"

"She drowned when I was five."

That word, *drowned*, gave me a jolt, from Mario's baby, of course, but there seemed to be another drowning I ought to be remembering.

The waiter returned with a bottle of wine and a wooden-handled deep-sea corkscrew. He screwed it in and popped the cork and poured the wine for me, but all I could think was, Forget this sexist formality and let's get on with the drinking that will hopefully loosen the tongue of the drinker.

Kirsten watched the waiter walk away. She said, "The question is, does he choose to mince away like that? Why did he choose to work in a macho-style place of employment? I'll tell you, since you were asking. The subconscious is the ocean. The paddles in our lifeboats are of little use against the currents that take us here and there. That's from the I Ching, you know, the bone-throwing book."

I sat back and stared at her, still waiting for the confession.

"Is my level of discourse too deep for you, dude? Let's say the waiter is gay, meaning he's been adrift most of his life. Maybe now he's become the adult he was meant to be."

Now she was staring at me, as though she expected an intelligent response. I said, "Your mother killed the adult you could have become. I don't understand that."

Her eyes slid away, back to the water. "When I was about twelve, across the street from my Aunt Bessie's house, a little girl played all day in the front yard. Every day I watched her playing. Everything she did was fascinating. Everything she did was amazing, how she walked, not so much a walk but a series of skips. She had a little baby carriage and had dolls that she looked after all day and she had little teacups and plates and served them milk and cookies. So, I said to Aunt Bessie, 'I'm sure this little girl is no different from any other little girls, so why do I find her so amazing?' Aunt Bessie said, 'Because she's so much like how you could have been if you had been able to be a little girl.'"

I waited.

"It's the bad stuff from childhood lodged in your subconscious that makes you the adult you've become rather than the adult you were meant to be. I used to watch my mother at the kitchen counter with a measuring cup and a little bottle of something that she had opened. She held it in her left hand and used an eyedropper to suck up the stuff in the bottle. She had to squirt some back and then she sucked up a little more. She seemed to have trouble getting the right amount before she squirted it into the measuring cup. She put the cap on the bottle and put it into the pocket of her blue jeans. She poured the stuff in the measuring cup into a pot of what might have been soup, or, I don't know, whatever you cook in a pot. It was some kind of Chinese healing recipe made from fish guts. I can still see her doing that. I can see the tip of her tongue slide along the white enamel of her teeth to make 'the' and 'k' when she said the name of the stuff she was making."

"What was the stuff in the eyedropper?"

"Hash oil, dude. Marijuana. She was stoned all the time."

The daisy arrived with the bottle of wine. I ordered the chicken special for us both, and we settled back with our drinks. My eyes wandered from the view across the table to the view out the window. In the foreground, the sailboats were moored, and in the background, Lake Ontario sparkled in a setting sun. This clear flat blue picture brought me back to Kirsten's blue-sky medallion, tangled in the worms on the bare skin of her neck.

Ordinarily, I would be thinking: drink some wine, enjoy the view, enjoy the meal, go home, watch the news, go to bed. That was how dinner at Sailor's used to start and that was how it used to end and that was how this evening should end, but for the fact that this was Kirsten sitting there, like a phone call received but not understood, or like an email sent that could not be opened. There she was, looking over the water and the sky which came together where the flat earth ended. She was wearing that same look she wore when she was studying her Tarot cards, so I knew that the dingbat occult craziness that was coming would be not a confession but a conundrum. In a minute, she'd tell me what the water was telling the sky to tell her to tell me.

She said, "Did you see that movie where this couple, they weren't a couple, just sort of hung out together, but one night they got drunk and next morning woke up married?"

"No kidding?"

"Kidding, yes. But what would happen if it turned out this couple that got drunk were related? Was he her uncle or something like that? Life has a funny way of taking you where it wants you to go. Or, for example, a dude goes into a lap-dance bar and it turns out the lap dancer is his daughter he never met because he checked out before she was born. That's why I check my horoscope, to read the signs and be ready for the unexpected. For example, a note left in a bible is a sign. Mrs. Ex's lover had a bible lying there. Normal for a priest, but you picked it up, not normal for you, and you found a note that changed your life. The unexpected that changed your life had been brewing like fish-gut soup in a pot you didn't know existed. At Lois's house, you picked up the bible. You could have picked up almost anything else. But again, you picked up the bible. In it, again, you found a message, this time from Reverend Beachy."

Daisy set down the steaming chicken dinner. Not even a Duck would use catsup on this fantastic presentation. Kirsten picked up her fork and positioned it between thumb and forefinger and held it like Martha Stewart between bites, her wrist resting on the edge of the table, her face turned to the window, her eyes taking in yachts and sailboats lined up under a setting sun. Definitely no catsup about this girl.

I was now into my third glass of wine. I sat back, not to watch her eat, dainty as a daisy, but to try and see what else there was in the rays of evening sun bouncing off the flat blue water of Lake Ontario and glinting across the surface of that karma thing as it swung back and forth with the movement of her arm picking up her glass.

Daisy arrived with an Academy-Award pepper mill and, with a twist of the hip, ground fresh pepper onto each plate. I felt my eyes fasten on the blue of the stone, drawing me in like the eyes of the statue. "Where did you get that thing?"

Her glass suspended, she stared not at me but past me, her line of sight directed over my shoulder and across the water. I didn't know for sure that she was going to reveal something important, but at the same time, I did.

She said, "My mother got permission from the state of Texas to watch the execution of her biker boss who killed three strippers. She got a front-row seat, that's how much she hated him. Aunt Bessie went with her. Nine o'clock in the morning he was the first one up. He had blue eyes, Bessie said. The execution room was empty except for a flat aluminum gurney with one white sheet and one white pillow beside the black machine with black wires crisscrossed across the front."

She was reciting the story, as though she had played it back to herself many times.

"They helped him onto the gurney. He lay back on the pillow, his feet stretched out, his arms at his sides, all four fastened. While one attendant tucked a draw sheet across his chest, a second fastened a belt across his legs and a third inserted the mouthpiece. A fourth unwrapped two pencil-like electrodes with flat, flanged bases and smeared on contact jelly while a fifth pressed the electrodes against his temple and stood back for the doctor to insert the drugs into the IV drip.

"Then with a jolt his body tightened and then, as the current pulsed into his heart and his legs went jerky and his toes and the arches of his feet curled inward, he looked straight at my mother and their eyes locked at the exact minute his body began to thrash about. After forty-five seconds, the convulsions stopped and he sank back down on the sheet.

"They went home. Bessie said my mother stayed in bed for a week. She wouldn't eat or drink and wouldn't let Bessie call 911. The neighbour down the hall knew of a priest with special powers. So, Bessie phoned him. He said, 'I will need three candles.'

"Bessie said she watched the priest pull up to the front of the house. He climbed the front steps and knocked. Bessie opened the door and led the way through the kitchen to the back bedroom. He stood by my mother's bed. Her eyes were closed, her hair spread out over the pillow. 'I have to light three candles,' the priest said to Aunt Bessie. 'It's better if she can light them, but if she can't, I will do it for her.'

"The priest lit them. When he placed his palm on her forehead, my mother's eyes opened. Her eyes met his for a moment, not for long, but long enough for him to see into their depth and to measure the reach required to draw from him what she needed.

"Afterward, having put out the candles, all but one of which he gave to Bessie, he left the room and went out onto the porch. Bessie came down the steps and stood on the sidewalk at a pace in front of him. It was dark and she stood before him. In the light from the candle, which was casting a shadow along the lines in his face, Bessie saw that he had blue eyes, not unusual except they had darker-blue flecks in them, like marbles, exactly the same as the executed biker.

"Bessie asked, 'How much do I owe you for coming?' The priest said, 'There is no charge.' Bessie said, 'I have some money.' The priest said, 'No. There is no charge.' Bessie insisted. 'But I have to pay you for what you did.'

"The priest said, 'I did nothing. Healings are all around us, happening at every minute. Sometimes the inner doctor just needs a gentle nudge.' Bessie asked, 'She's all better now?' The priest said, 'That's up to her.'

"Bessie said that when my mother looked into the eyes of the biker she saw only evil, and then when she looked into the eyes of the priest she saw only good... So, after that, Bessie said, my mother started studying the occult and making that fish-gut soup, and wearing karma stuff, trying to get to that place she'd seen in the priest's eyes and away from the place she'd seen in the biker's eyes. And that changed her life. She stopped stripping. She got a job waitressing. She got a decent boyfriend who had a sailboat. Stone sober, the water as still and flat as it is now, my mother fell overboard and drowned. I inherited all her occult stuff, including this karma thing."

She was looking across the water and when I looked, I knew she saw the water's two different blues.

She said, "Track it backward. There is always a pot somewhere brewing you a surprise that will change your life. Think for a moment. Pause for a moment's reflection. Here we are on the shore of the flat blue water. But in its underwater currents are two separate pairs of eyes that are both blue, but two different blues."

I drank my wine; Kirsten sipped hers, her little finger cocked. "I don't want to end up like my mother. I'm a hard worker, I have a good attitude and, as you already know, I will be a benefit to your business."

Kirsten went back to eating, staring at me, nibbling at her dinner the way she nibbled at my mind, the way she nibbled at my emotions. She said, "I will tell Reverend Beachy I'm getting married, then I will shift the conversation to Lois, whom I might ask to sew the wedding dress. From there, I will lead Reverend Beachy into a conversation in which he will tell us everything he knows about Lois, like where she came from, and her family background, stuff like that."

What I thought was, what I imagined was, her standing before the reverend in her white wedding dress with one of those bride things holding down her hair.

She continued. "What choice do you have? If you go to see Reverend Beachy without me, how much information do you think he'll give you?"

I knew she was right. She had conned Lenssen into giving her the picture of the Gabriella statue, and now she was figuring out a way to con the reverend for information on Lois, and then I thought, I'm as gullible as the other two. And this made me feel uncomfortable to the point of doubting what sounded like a rehearsed story about her mother going to an execution. Then I thought about the same-coloured eyes being opposites. Then I thought about the innocent blue eyes of Mario's baby that had not had a chance to choose a direction. Then I thought, I need another glass of wine.

Chapter Twelve

The morning after our dinner at Sailor's, Kirsten appeared for breakfast in her usual bathrobe with cats and PJs with dogs. I was seated at the kitchen table writing up a contract on my laptop for the Shepherd Foundation.

Kirsten sat opposite me. "So, what made you decide?"

"Your story about blue-eyed good and evil. Mario's baby had blue eyes. That karma thing you always wear that's always looking at me has blue eyes. Maybe those missing children had blue eyes. The fact is, if the mothers believe their missing children are still with them, still calling to them, although the voices of the children grow fainter, those voices will never fade away, and neither will the blue of their eyes."

"Sounds poetic, dude. Poetic but true."

Kirsten plugged in the kettle and opened the top cupboard for one of her Tazo Organic Chai Black Weirdness teabags. She poured her tea into a Tim Hortons mug that Mrs. Ex had packed away out of sight years ago. She sat opposite me, looking into her tea. She said, "The Lazore family disappeared in June. The three girls disappeared in June. This is June. Make an appointment with Reverend Beachy, see what he has to say about Lois."

"Reverend Beachy will protect his parishioners. He'll tell me nothing."

"Dude, I told you, that's why you need the help of the associate you just hired."

With her little finger cocked like teatime with the Queen, she said, "Here's another idea. I will go undercover. I will find a way to get inside the Lazore and look around and give you another reading."

"And if you get caught?"

"I'll pretend I wanted to rent a room. I'll say, I heard there might be a vacancy, so I thought I'd I have a quick peek. Oh my, yes, and what an interesting old house. But no one answered my knock, so I tried the door and oh my goodness, it wasn't locked."

Kirsten returned to the kitchen for more tea in her Tim Hortons mug. She stood at the counter, one hand on her hip, the other stirring in the sugar. She placed the mug on the table and went upstairs. She returned in ten minutes looking like a street kid, dressed in a short-sleeve T-shirt and ordinary jeans. There was that about her. She could go undercover as a fifteen-year-old kid trying to rent a room. She could go undercover in a bar trapping cheaters. She could con anyone into anything.

Except, the undercover idea returned me to that other thought that was bugging me. She had only one suitcase when she moved in, nothing more. Yet she had this endless supply of clothes picked up at Goodwill, she said. "No bed bugs or roaches, I hope," I had said, and she'd given me her attitude, leaving me with an unanswered question: does she have another apartment that she'll move back to when she feels safe? That would explain the difficulty with paying the rent. This would be the logical explanation.

Kirsten said, "Let's go check out the Lazore. We park around the corner. I'll see if anyone is there to rent me a room, which there won't be. If I get in, I'll phone you."

"No, I'll go with you. We look around outside. We look in the windows. We do not break in."

As we were coming up the sidewalk, Kirsten walking ahead of me, a fat balding man was leaving the house next door. Since he made no effort to make room to pass, Kirsten had to step aside. The man outweighed me by a hundred pounds but I anticipated the collision and leaned in and knocked the man off the sidewalk. "So sorry," I apologized.

Kirsten helped the man up. "Why did you do that? Jeez, dude. What is the matter with you? You don't have to raise your leg on everyone bigger than you."

The man muttered something.

Kirsten said, "You must live close by, Mr...."

"Balinski."

He stared at me. I said, "I apologize. I'm sorry."

Kirsten said, "He's sorry."

With random slaps, she helped Mr. Balinski brush himself off. "I can't take him anywhere. Bull in a china shop. I can't teach him anything. He's lost his filters. He should be in an institution, on the dribbler ward. There, that's better."

Kirsten pointed at the Lazore. "What a spooky place to have next door. Does it give you the creeps, you know, at night with a full moon and the wind moving the trees in the shadows?"

Mr. Balinski glanced at the Lazore. "I sometimes think I see someone walking around in there at night. But I think it's from the street lights reflecting on the glass. That's why people say it's haunted."

Mr. Balinski continued down the street. I followed Kirsten to the rear of the property. Kirsten *tap-tapped* on the door.

Kirsten said, "I think I heard someone call, 'Come in.' Maybe I'm mistaken. I'll check around the front."

I was not surprised when, five minutes later, the door swung open.

"How did you do that?"

"Better you don't know. I don't want you to lose your license now that I'm a paid employee."

We followed a musty hallway into a kitchen, fully equipped with a fridge, stove, table, chairs, and in the cupboards and drawers, dishes, pots, cutlery.

"But no power," I said, flipping the light switch.

Kirsten wandered into the living room, fully furnished with matching chesterfield and chairs, and an ancient TV that dated the family's departure from the Lazore back to the sixties.

Kirsten examined the framed photograph of Gabriella hanging on the wall; she stared back with empty eyes. Then Kirsten went into the hall to look at the photograph suspended at a slant of baby Isabela dressed in a sleeper and bonnet, lying in a bassinette. Kirsten wandered farther along the hall and stopped to look at another picture of the baby Isabela. She went to the next, fat Mrs. Lazore seated in a high-backed chair holding the baby with the doctor behind her, hands gripping the edge of the chair as though he were hanging on trying to keep himself upright. He was as skinny as she was fat, but not as thin as Gabriella standing next to him, her spindle arms sticking out of a shapeless dress.

Kirsten came back to the living room doorway. She stood, hands on her hips, foot tapping, looking at Gabriella. "She looks dead already, and Mr. and Mrs. Lazore... No one is smiling, no joy on their blank faces."

Kirsten went again from picture to picture and stopped at the doctor. "Where is your baby, Dr. Lazore? Tell me now, tell me later. Makes no difference to me. I'll find out eventually."

She checked her watch and said to the picture, "I should be on my way to work. I don't need a ride, Dr. Lazore. It's been a spooky pleasure. I will be back."

I drove slowly; Kirsten was quiet, staring out the window.

I said, "What do you think?"

"I think there were no dead mice on the floor, no dead flies on the windowsill, no cobwebs hanging in corners. Someone's been keeping it clean."

Kirsten became reflective, hands in her lap, the thumb of her right hand stroking along the back of her left, an insignificant gesture, I realized, but so familiar it shouted, "Remember me, Quinn?"

Kirsten said, "While I was staring at Gabriella, studying her face, it was like looking at one of those inkblot pictures, you know. What does your mind see in this inkblot?"

"What did you see?"

"The Lazore back window looks directly across to Lois's kitchen window. If I had strong enough binoculars, I would be able to see into Lois's eyes and I would see evil, like my mother saw evil in that biker's eyes. The evil I would see is that Lois sneaks across the backyard into the basement through those hurricane doors to visit Isabela lying under the concrete floor."

When we arrived home, instead of going upstairs to get ready for work, Kirsten plunked herself down on the chesterfield. I sat beside her.

She said, "When I was looking out the Lazore kitchen window it felt like I was standing in a fog. If I looked one way, what was in front of me was too foggy to see clearly, and if I looked the other way, what was ahead was too foggy to see clearly. But I had the feeling that the fingers of Gabriella in the photo on the wall of the Lazore were holding a thread that stretched through the window to Lois, one end of the fog to the other. If I had infrared fog-penetrating binoculars, I could see that thread and all the other threads like straight lines going directly from Lois to Isabela and the three missing girls."

I remembered working stakeouts, sitting behind strip clubs with Night Owls, on the lookout for drug violations by the bikers. I was never concerned about what the girls were doing in the club. They were just trying to make a living. I'd never heard of infrared fog-penetrating binoculars but imagined they'd come in handy for tracking cheaters.

She said, "Lois reminds me of Aunt Bessie, not her looks but the look on her face, like she's hiding something. Aunt Bessie played dumb about my father. I'd ask her about him and her face would get a blank look. She told me he worked shifts. He chewed gum because he was drinking on the job. He'd throw the gum wrappers all over the place, she said. Then a few days later, talking about something else, she'd say he didn't drink, ever. So, I knew she was hiding something."

In vice, I'd met hundreds of strippers. They came and they went. Although there was a lot of drinking — too many times my mind was fogged with alcohol — my brain must have been keeping a log. That would explain my Alzheimer's déjà vu, remembering but not remembering, both at the same time. Kirsten was handing me another snapshot of her background, one at a time, it seemed, and eventually, as the pictures began to line up, I would be able to follow them back one at a time, yes, like following a thread backward, one step at a time, and there she would be. But so what? I never had any real connection to the dancers. It was the bikers me and Parsons were after, never the girls.

Kirsten got up. I watched the too-familiar swing of her step as she walked away, and although she was only going to the door of her upstairs apartment ten feet away, I had the feeling you get when you need to catch up to someone and either go with them or bring them back before it's too late, and they're gone.

Chapter Thirteen

Kirsten was busy at the kitchen counter making lunch. She was wearing one of my Raptors T-shirts, which was hanging almost to the knees of her black tights.

"Lunch is a baked omelet," she said, wiping her hands on a tea towel as she was coming into my spare bedroom-office to look over my shoulder at the original side-by-side photo of Gabriella and her father next to its reproduction.

She said, "Look at Gabriella's eyes in the reprint."

I opened my desk drawer, cleaned my magnifying glass with my tie, and squinted through the lens, raising and lowering it until I had a clear image.

She said, "It's an optical illusion, but the eyes look luminous, as if they can see us."

I now recognized that the photograph had been taken in the side yard of the Lazore, for the background was a stone foundation wall with one small basement window.

"There's the baby." Kirsten pointed one long red nail.

Sure enough, in the reflection from the glass of the window lay a baby on a blanket in the grass.

Kirsten asked, "So why would someone take a photo of Gabriella and the doctor standing against the wall and leave the baby lying in the grass? Someone should be holding the baby."

"The photographer put down the baby to take the photo," I suggested.

"That baby's dead; the blanket is covering its face."

I looked more closely. "I think you're jumping to conclusions. I think you might cover a baby's face for other reasons, bugs for example. And why, if you've got a dead baby to deal with, would you be thinking about taking a photograph?"

"I'm just saying what it looks like. That's what eyes do, they tell you what stuff looks like."

"Who is taking the picture?"

"The mother. She set the dead baby in the grass to take the picture. Can you get that reflection part blown up?"

She stood back, waiting for my answer.

I said, "I had a case once, the perv photographed his victim. In one picture, the reflection in the eyes of the vic identified the perpetrator. Too bad I can't give this to Parsons for forensics."

"Why can't you? It's cop stuff. You worked the streets together. Take a bullet for your partner, like in the movies."

"My old partner helped solved this case. I'm not interested in proving him wrong."

"But that's what we're doing."

"I'm proving him right. And I'm giving closure to the parents who are haunted by the idea that the police were wrong and the bodies of the children are buried somewhere on the Lazore property, sitting there every day in a yard full of weeds and coming to them every night in their dreams. I'm giving them closure."

The oven timer buzzed, a feature I did not know I had. Kirsten hurried away. In a few minutes, she called me for lunch. It smelled delicious, and with the cheese and mushroom topping, it looked professionally made.

"How did you do this?" I didn't know I had anything to eat in the fridge, except leftover chicken.

"I used what I found: eggs, cheese, mushrooms, cooked ham. All of it left over from when you went to high school."

"You know how to cook, you're telling me."

"I've worked all my adult life in restaurants. Of course I know how to cook. Hurry up and eat. The way you drive we'll be late for Reverend Beachy. And wear something appropriate."

I was standing at the bathroom mirror adjusting my two-tone blue tie when she returned from upstairs, appropriately dressed in a blouse and white capris.

"Very nice," I said. She stood beside me and began beating at her hair with her brush, apparently trying to put it in a style suitable for visiting a reverend. At the same time, she was giving me non-verbal criticisms by way of sideways glances at my shirt/tie/jacket combo.

I looked down at my clothes. "What's the matter with them?"

"I didn't say anything."

"You don't like the tie."

"Would look great if this was 1970."

"My ties are all 1970."

"You look like a cop wearing a blue-striped tie, brown tweed jacket, and grey shirt. As soon as I saw you that first day on your doorstop, lost and penniless, I said to myself: cop."

I felt another far away jolt. "Why when you first saw me were you already thinking cop?"

"Only businessmen and detectives wear suits, but a businessman would never wear a 1970s tie."

I took it off.

She gave up on the hair and took over on the tie. "What are you going to ask the reverend?"

"Good question. If I say I'm a detective, he won't tell me anything."

"Then let me ask the questions. You keep quiet."

She had lifted my shirt collar and was concentrating on positioning the tie, her fingers smoothing it along the back of my neck. This was another question needing an answer. Yes, her familiarity was part of how she was and she was using it to get what she wanted, not only free rent but also protection and a job. But there was an innocence about this familiarity that suggested that she considered her relaxed closeness as both normal and natural, as though I was some harmless uncle, just as she had walked into my apartment and, in a normal and natural way, made herself right at home, as though she actually felt she belonged there.

Still busy with the tie, she said, "I'm thinking of getting married and need a reverend to do the deed and we're thinking of moving into the area and the real estate lady said Lois might be selling her house and what does he, the reverend, know about Lois and so on and stuff like that."

I knew she would make it work.

She did the loop over and slipped the knot tight and stood back to look.

Reverend Beachy's address was a manse on a tree-lined street next to the Presbyterian church. The reverend was wearing his white collar and black clerics. After a warm handshake, he ushered Kirsten and me into the living room and offered coffee.

Kirsten got right down to business. "We're thinking of getting married and I had some sewing done by Lois Miller and she suggested we see you."

Reverend Beachy glanced at me, now sunk into the springs of the soft living room chair, no doubt worn out by fat church ladies. Reverend Beachy's glance became a scowl. No doubt he was thinking: Is this young bride perched on the edge of her chair looking vibrantly beautiful going to marry *him*?

I did not correct this assumption, for Kirsten was now wearing her familiar cutsie coy smile as the wheels and belts in her mind meshed together a spontaneous series of lies to feed the reverend.

"There are a lot of difficult issues to deal with before you get married so we were talking to Lois and she said we should talk to you."

"Yes," said the reverend, nodding and smiling, already falling in love with Kirsten, already looking forward to performing the ceremony.

Kirsten continued, "My Aunt Bessie always said men are good for lifting heavy stuff and sometimes good for killing spiders but not much else. He'll be good at the lifting part but I don't know about the spiders."

"I have a joke," said the reverend, leaning forward, the two of them already close friends. "It doesn't matter how often a married man changes jobs, he still ends up with the same boss."

He smiled at me. I smiled back.

"We don't want to get it wrong," continued the bride. "He's older, I know, but we've known one another for years and, you know, it's almost like the Lord has this planned for us. Quinn's been my rock and protector all these years. Like the bible quote: 'I have made you and I will carry you; I will sustain you and I will rescue you.'"

"Isaiah 46:4," said the reverend, beaming a pious smile.

"Aunt Bessie would say you can't blame everything on your husband and you can't blame everything on the government so before you get into marriage, you better get your head straight about taking some of the blame yourself."

"A wise woman," said the reverend.

"Talking about finances, we were looking for houses in the area and Lois said hers might soon be for sale. Is she having health issues? I know my Aunt Bessie had to sell her house when her health failed, God rest her soul."

"Yes, God rest her soul. I don't know about real estate, but yes, I do hold pre-marriage courses. You're welcome to join."

The reverend disappeared into his kitchen and returned with a marriage pamphlet. He gave it to Kirsten, who said, "Back to Lois Miller. I had some sewing done by her and I thought she seemed a little distracted."

The reverend hesitated. His face became pulpit-solemn, as though he was not certain how to phrase his answer without first checking with God. Finally, he said, "A lonely woman all by herself, poor soul. She has what started off as a hobby making rag dolls but I'm beginning to wonder about early Alzheimer's. The dolls have long been her only company, which was fine for a time, except now, the way she talks, I'm beginning to think they have taken on a life of their own. So yes, I'm pleased to learn she is thinking about selling. Hopefully she'll choose assisted living."

"What do you mean, a life of their own?"

Reverend Beachy extended his hands and flexed his fingers. "As well as taking in sewing, she is constantly sewing dolls so that now she has calluses and cuts on these two fingers." He held them up. "I don't know, but without going into detail, she seems to think the dolls are real people, and she seems to have some kind of punishment obsession with the constant sewing."

"Like Lady Macbeth," said Kirsten.

"Yes, yes, the hands washing the sin away."

"Or punishing the hands for the sin." Kirsten's face showed concern. "But living alone, you know, my grandfather, a handyman guy, after his wife died, he spent all his time in his workshop sorting different sized screws into jars. He'd sort them all and then, when he was finished, he'd dump them on the workbench and start all over again."

The reverend nodded. "Perhaps he'd forgotten he'd already done them, which would suggest Alzheimer's."

I thought, That sounds like me, like why are these screws looking familiar?

"I'll be seeing Lois soon, Reverend Beachy, so I can keep you informed."

Kirsten got up and I stood next to her.

At the door, Kirsten hesitated. "The dolls. A life of their own? That is troubling."

The reverend in a sad voice said, "She wondered if I would perform funeral services for them."

"You mean she thinks they die? Does she think she's killing them?"

"I don't know, but like your grandfather, her mind could be going. Not unusual, it seems, these days."

Kirsten thanked the reverend, promised to attend the next pre-marriage class, and we left.

"You didn't give me a chance to ask any questions," I said when we were back in the car.

"I didn't need to. I was magnificent. She's making Isabela dolls and then 'killing' them. Now I know for sure those three little girls are buried in the Lazore yard. Add a pair of Presbyterian wings to the statue and you've got Gabriella's graveyard. And I can prove it if I go back to the Lazore and look at the family pictures again." Kirsten checked her watch. "But not now. I have to go to work."

I took a left and parked at my house. I waited on the chesterfield while she got ready for her shift at the Deuce. She returned in a few minutes wearing her distressed jeans and a blue sweater.

We drove in silence to the Deuce. It was a clear mid-June day, the sun hot on the window. I thought about turning on the AC but I was enjoying the aroma of shampoo combined with something else that reminded me of midnight raids on the holistic therapy clinic on Sherbourne Street. The smell of incense was pleasant. But what was going on there was not. As Parsons and I had cuffed the three scumbags we'd apprehended, Parsons said to the three makeup-covered sixteen-year-olds working there, "Take it off before I take you home. It's called a face, not a colouring book."

With this memory stuck in my mind I checked the Deuce parking lot as I pulled up, but there were no Harleys.

As I eased into an empty spot, my cell rang. I listened and hung up. "That was Parsons. Another little girl went missing, this time from a Howland address behind the Lazore. They've got another nanny. Parsons was right."

Kirsten stared at me, frowned at me. "No, Parsons was wrong. The nanny he caught can't have kidnapped this girl, she's in prison."

"Well, yeah, maybe it's a different nanny from the same cartel."

The evening news was filled with cop-speak about missing children, community confidence, coming forward, a twenty-four-hour window, and a photograph of the little girl called Emily, along with a 1-800 phone number, approximate time of disappearance, and a description of what she was wearing. The news clip showed the police searching the area with sniffer dogs.

I said, "I don't want to watch this."

Kirsten said, "I want another look at those Lazore family pictures hanging on the wall."

"It's an open case now, so no, you can't go there and snoop around."

"I'm going anyway."

I pretended indifference with a shrug. I knew she should keep her nose out of it but I didn't want my "Adventures with Kirsten" to end. Neither did I want to get involved with another murdered child. Not this time. That's why I retired. No more Lazore for me.

Chapter Fourteen

But with the disappearance of the fourth little girl, Kirsten's persistence became an obsession. I did not know how many times Kirsten had, before or after or partway through her shifts at the Deuce, gone into the Lazore through the side window off the pantry. And now, despite my better judgment, there I was standing in the Lazore living room while Kirsten gave me her official reading.

"These pictures have the answer. It's bad luck to leave your pictures hanging on the wall; they'll cast spells on the person who moves in. That's why the spooks and the spirits are trying to help me. They're here trying to tell me what happened. I can smell them, like burnt cookies. Their energy is transmitted on higher wavelengths that heat up surrounding molecules. You usually can't smell it, but in here there's no circulation of fresh air."

Kirsten stopped at a faded square on the wall. "Gabriella took this one down. Or at least someone did. If you take only one down and leave the rest up, that's a sign you're trying to hide something."

She moved to the next one. "What do you think about losing some weight, Mrs. Lazore? You feed yourself but you don't feed your own children. Look at Gabriella, thin as a bean pole."

She went to the next photograph, where Dr. Lazore was seated in his big chair for another family portrait. "What were you looking at, Dr. Lazore? What I'm looking at now must be the same as what you would be looking at if you could see: the living room with the chesterfield backed against the window and on one side the red easy chair and on the other side the blue easy chair and straight ahead the television.

"In this one, what Gabriella was looking at then would be the same as what I'm looking at now. Down the hall is to the laundry room. To the left, the doorway to the kitchen; to the right, the back door. By following Gabriella's line of sight, I can see that Gabriella would be looking not at another picture, but the blank square. Why did they take that one picture and not the others?"

Kirsten waited, then answered: "Because that blank square wasn't a picture; it was a mirror."

I said, "Why take the mirror?"

"You need a mirror. You don't need a picture. But there's another reason. The mirror is a particular example of the universal sky that is watching and recording and reflecting universal karma. The mirror watches and records and reflects *individual* karma. When you look into the mirror, what do you see reflecting back to you? Yourself. Lois, the adult Gabriella, doesn't want the child Gabriella, who is hanging across from the mirror, reflecting on herself. Lois has either broken it or hidden it."

Kirsten moved on. "Here's another of the whole family. There is the wee baby Isabela. She doesn't look too happy. Aunt Bessie would say, 'Give that baby a rum sour, for her gums.' The I Ching says it's bad luck to throw away pictures of dead babies because if you do, they come back to you at night when you're sleeping. First you smell the burnt cookies and then you hear them say, 'What did you do with my pictures?' See this one of Isabela? How would you like it if she came back to you while you were sleeping and said, 'What did you do with my pictures?'"

I wanted to say my dead baby already does come back to me while I'm sleeping but Kirsten continued. "Lois has an occult symbol on her front door. Why? To prevent Isabela from getting in. She probably has one on her back door. Besides, Dr. Lazore was a psychiatrist in the sixties, which means he was only one notch above a witch doctor. Who knows what sort of nonsense he was feeding Gabriella about spooks and spirits and dead people."

Kirsten was staring at the blank square, as though she was looking into the mirror. "In the basement window, what did we see? The reflection of the dead baby. If we find the missing mirror, what will we see?"

Now I felt like I was back in the morgue, listening to a coroner explain the cause of death as I pulled back the sheet. The coroner used the same kind of logic as Kirsten was using to explain how this wound meant one thing and this bruise meant some other thing.

I was thankful when Kirsten left the pictures and went over to stand in the daylight coming through the front window. She was finished, I hoped, ready to leave this eerie place that kept stirring up the muddy waters.

No such luck.

"Gabriella's statue spends all day standing there looking at the street. She's watching the kids coming home from the elementary school. They know she's watching them so they cross over to the other side, afraid they're next on her list. I noticed them doing that, so I asked one little girl about it. She said the house is haunted. I asked why she thought that. She said, 'In the reflection in the front window you can see ghosts.' Which is the same as what Mr. Balinski said."

I followed her along the hall to the doctor's office: two corner windows, one looking onto the backyard and one onto the side yard. In the photograph over his desk, Gabriella in her pale dress and dark knee socks was standing in the backyard, her back to the window and the camera. In the picture, the back lawn was all weeds, the same as now. At the back of the property was the board fence, the same as now. What was not the same as now was the path ending at the missing board. Kirsten would in her mind turn that picture around and, from the opposite direction, see that missing board as a doorway opening up to a path leading directly to the statue where, according to Kirsten, the little girls were buried. Then for confirmation of this fact she would point to the tree, off to one side. In the picture it was alive. Now it was dead, its roots damaged, presumably by the burying of the little girl. Which might account for the inability for the radar to find the little girls. When I mentioned this to Kirsten she said, "I already checked that out. The machine takes tree roots into account… What we need are binoculars, the best you can buy."

As usual, she was three steps ahead of me. No one had ever been three steps ahead of me on the force, well, apart from Parsons — usually there were four or five pairs of eyes on everything, so no one needed to notice every detail. And no one could go off on the wild tangents that allowed Kirsten to notice the kinds of things she did.

She said, "Can I go to a pawnshop and buy the best set of binoculars they've got?"

I gave her the money.

Chapter Fifteen

I arrived at the Lazore just before dark and ducked under the yellow tape. Kirsten answered my knock on the back door. I smelled her shampoo; at least I thought that's what I was smelling. It was difficult to tell, mixed with the smell of burnt cookies. She was staring at a photograph of Mrs. Lazore, who was staring straight back.

Kirsten said, "Three summers ago a neighbour left her baby in the car by accident. The baby suffocated. The mother blamed herself. She couldn't let it go. I talked to her the day before she committed suicide. I could see it in her eyes; remember, I told you how my mother could see stuff in people's eyes. Mrs. Lazore had that look in her eyes when this picture was taken. So, she was thinking about suicide but then, change of plans, Gabriella killed the baby."

I left her looking at the photographs and took the new binoculars and went to the back window and peered across the yard at the cross symbol hanging on the back door of Lois's house. I slid my vision along the fence and through the kitchen window. She was seated at her sewing machine. Behind her, on a wooden drying rack, hung what looked like a child's jumper. But no, it could be anything hanging on that drying rack. I fixed on the sewing machine. I fixed on the high-speed needle laying down its tiny stitches. I fixed on Lois's hands, busy on a new doll. I fixed on Lois's face, scowling at the little feet as she worked, careful not to stick herself with the pins that she kept in the pincushion next to the silver thing for her fingertip. In one corner on the floor lay what looked like a child's blue hairclip. I closed one eye for a better focus. But no. It looked more like a length of folded wool.

Standing back one-eyed through the round window, I could almost see the ghost of Gabriella hanging over Lois's shoulder, scheming a way to pick up that blue wool, ghosts not having fingers. At least, I didn't think they would. I handed the binoculars to Kirsten, who adjusted the focus. "Lois just checked her watch. She's setting the doll aside and going to the kitchen counter and taking out a plate. Now she's opening the refrigerator and taking out sandwiches wrapped in cellophane and a bowl of red stuff that looks like Jell-O. She's opening the door next to the refrigerator, it looks like a pantry … ohmygosh holy smokes, on the other side of the door hanging on the wall, it's the mirror!"

I said, "Check out the symbol on the back door."

She focused on the symbol. "It's a serpent cross, the cross is right-side up, yes but wrapped around it, you almost can't see it, is a serpent upside down."

She put down the binoculars. Her lips were a little parted, like she had all the answers ready on the tip of her tongue, which was feeling along the edges of her top front teeth, preparing to deliver her conclusions.

She said, "I brought Lois's face right up close, right up to mine. Those same blank eyes were showing no emotion, the same as the blank eyes of the statue. The eyes are the window to the soul, dude. Remember I told you about the execution of the biker? Gabriella was a psychopath back then living here in this house and is a psychopath now living over there on Howland. And that hairclip on the floor is decorated with little ducks, so it belongs to a little girl. It's Emily's, I'm sure of it."

"That wasn't a hair clip. It was a piece of wool."

Binoculars fixed, Kirsten took a second look. "Yeah. I think you're right."

My cell phone rang. I listened and hung up. "Parsons says it's Emily's nanny, working with her uncle. It looks like they lured Emily away by promising her a trip to Disneyland. They aren't sure where this place they're calling Disneyland is, could be close by. They've searched all the neighbouring houses top to bottom including Lois's. Top to bottom. They've searched the Lazore too, must have been when we weren't here."

Kirsten's answer was not immediate. I waited. Finally, she said, "I know you don't want me to talk about a missing little girl. It stirs up too many memories. But the thing is, dude, you couldn't save the last one but you might be able to save this one."

"Perhaps. But the police have checked out all the neighbours, including Lois. For the time being the Lazore is off limits. Yellow tape. It's a police investigation. Besides, according to your theory, Lois is burying the bodies in the side yard. This means she'll keep little Emily alive until all this activity is over and she's free to dig."

Kirsten had no answer, which, as far as I was concerned, meant she thought I was right. That is, until she began to circle the room, her strange internal scanners measuring and tabulating. "Nothing is out of place. If the police had done a thorough search, something would have been moved."

She checked each room. "But it doesn't matter. If Emily were here, I'd know it."

I knew Parsons was smarter than me, and so was Kirsten, way smarter, but she wasn't Parsons-smart, like remembering the batting average of every Blue Jay or what happened in 1897 or figuring out how long it would take if one car were travelling at sixty miles an hour and the other car at eighty, etc. and so on and so forth... Parsons was smart like that. But Kirsten had something else, as if her mind was dialed into different wavelengths and her brain picked up different signals, like how if you dial 1080 you get Country and Western but if you dial 1090 you get talk radio. But I had learned Parsons was never wrong. If his investigation concluded no little girl was buried on the Lazore property, I had to believe Parsons. Parsons was facts-based. Kirsten was conjecture-based. But fact and conjecture didn't matter because, for the time being, the Lazore was part of the police investigation. We couldn't cross the yellow tape.

Chapter Sixteen

On Saturday morning I stood before the bathroom mirror tying the green striped wool tie Kirsten had bought for me. She had come from her apartment, clumping down the stairs, looking like a sultry vixen in her clunky sandals and large dangly gold earrings and size six everything else. She had checked out the front window and then, through the open bathroom door, noticing me wrestling with my tie, trying to do my usual this over that, she came over and redid the knot.

She was six inches shorter than me, so my looking down, and her perfume drifting up, reminded me of my wife tying my tie in the early days before we got married, when we were still in love. I remembered thinking that the fact that I was older, the fact that my wife had been a flirt, confirmed my belief that her flirtation was about the biological drive for a protector, in my ex's case an abusive father. What had ended the marriage, however, was that other biological imperative: domination. And here I was on replay with Kirsten. Not only was she here for protection, but she had also taken over my house, my business, and my life.

I was beginning to think I needed counseling. There was relationship counseling, job counseling, retirement counseling. This would be ghost-from-the-past counseling.

The tie tied, she stepped back for a look, her head at an appraising incline. When I let her out at the Deuce ten minutes later, I said, "I need to do some work for a new client starting Monday. The husband figures while he's at work, his college professor wife is being visited by one of her students."

"So how will we catch the cheater?"

"It's usually easy, except this job is in the suburbs. I can't park in front of the house and wait for his visit without the nosy neighbours getting suspicious."

She was silent, which meant she had gone into her head, which was tilted in a familiar wheels-turning position, while the ambulatory computer called her brain created a plan.

She said, "I'm off Monday. I can spare you an hour. Wear your suit and tie and we can be Jehovah's Witnesses. We park the car, get out with our bibles, hang around, maybe knock on a door, go back to the car to arrange our pamphlets, wait for the lover to drive up. And when he does, we knock on her door and you sort of push our way in. You're good at that, and I'll make something up on the fly, I'm good at that. I will explain how Armageddon is about to happen, or whatever."

I dropped her off at the Deuce. As I detoured up Brunswick, I noticed the heavy man I had knocked over, Mr. Balinski, standing on the street examining the rear panel of a Hyundai.

I pulled over.

"Someone dinged the door," said Mr. Balinski. "He left a note: 'Sorry I dinged your car. I feel bad but not bad enough to offer to pay. It's my birthday and I was celebrating a bit. I know you wouldn't want to ruin my birthday.'"

"I'm guessing no signature."

"He must have been trying to park. And it must have been a pickup, his bumper's higher than mine."

"You must drive around here a lot. Ever notice anything suspicious next street over on Howland, the house backing onto the Lazore backyard?"

Mr. Balinski was still scowling at the dent. "He doesn't want to pay because it's his birthday."

I said, "I have a question to ask you. Who do you think took that little girl?"

"Why are you asking me?"

"Your best guess."

"I don't have a guess."

"Give me the first name that comes into your head."

"Why should I?"

"Give me a name and I'll tell you."

"Because I got a foreign name I kidnap little girls?"

"See? Balinski was the first name that came into your head when I asked the question."

"Fuck off."

"Don't leave town," I said.

"Horse shit."

Mr. Balinski got into his dinged-up car and drove off.

The Kirsten Method. Everyone almost sort of believed in psychic powers, not that anyone would admit it. But programs on TV and such, like *The Dog Whisperer*, if you pretend you've got the gift and plant the seeds of some bogus nonsense, people will believe it. The person you're investigating will begin to think you do in fact have special powers, like in *The Horse Whisperer* movie. That horse was guilty of something.

Chapter Seventeen

I said, "You suggested we pretend to be Jehovah's Witnesses, if I remember correctly."

"I will grace you with my presence but I want fifty per cent of the fee."

"Agreed. But you have to dress the part. No short shorts and tank tops that are good for nothing but causing gridlock on the street. And we have to go now. The husband left this afternoon on a business trip. When the cat's away and all that."

She disappeared upstairs and returned wearing a plain blouse, slacks, and flat shoes.

"We don't have any pamphlets," I said.

She went back to her apartment and returned with a King James Bible. "We don't need pamphlets."

In the car driving to the address, I asked, "You have your own bible. Did you get that in confirmation?"

"Yes. Catholic."

"How old were you when you got confirmed?"

"Twelve."

"When was that?"

"Yeah, right. I already told you my age, and don't say, 'Yes, but you're a compulsive liar.'"

While I navigated the traffic across the 401 to Leslie Street, instead of making smart cracks about my driving she leafed through the bible. "We have to have a line, like telemarketing. You can't just knock on the door and stand there and expect to be invited in. Something better than the usual scorched-earth stuff. Like, I will eloquently explain why Adam and Eve didn't have belly buttons. It says right here, he made Adam out of dirt, so, no belly buttons."

We arrived at the address on a street of row after row of perfect lawns and split-level sixties-style houses.

"We're in luck," I said. "The boyfriend drives a red Honda." I pointed to the car, a few doors down on the opposite of the street.

"So how do we do it?" I asked.

"You're the dumb one who stands there and doesn't say anything."

"I think you should be the dumb one."

"That would give it away. It's obvious that I'm the smart one."

We crossed the street, Kirsten carrying the bible. "My Aunt Bessie would say, 'Being a lifetime member of a church doesn't make you a Christian any more than a lifetime of driving makes you a car.'"

She gave me the bible to hold while she straightened my wool tie. She buttoned my suit jacket. "But dressing like a Jehovah's Witness might make you a Jehovah's Witness for a few minutes."

She stood back for a better look at me. "The Jehovah's men are usually skinny. After I introduce us, I'll say if you want to know how big Jehovah is, he's even bigger than him, and I'll point to you. But you can't say anything because you're the dumb one."

I stepped off the sidewalk to cut across the lawn, heading for the front door. She took my arm. "You are the dumb one. Don't you know you have to obey the path of the sidewalk when you're going door to door?"

I side-stepped onto the sidewalk.

Kirsten's knock was answered almost immediately by a young man wearing a Superman T-shirt, his hair messed up, the fly of his jeans undone. Kirsten opened the bible. "Would you like to learn about the *real* Superman?"

Behind the young man, an older woman appeared, tying her bathrobe.

"Gotcha," I muttered, my cell phone adding up the pictures in clicks.

Kirsten said, "You shouldn't have answered the door with your fly open."

I snapped a quick shot of the fly and, as we were leaving, another shot of the Honda's plates.

"That's all we have to do? I never got to explain who the real Superman was or why Adam and Eve didn't have belly buttons."

"Why didn't Adam and Eve have belly buttons?"

"Jesus, dude. They were created, not born. God shot off on a rock, and the sun hatched Adam and then God created Eve so Adam would have someone to tell him how to do stuff. They lived in the Garden of Eden, which was near what is now called the Speed Valley Parkway."

The mention of the Speed River gave me a jolt. Kirsten paused. She gave me her sideways-slanted questioning stare. She said, "Sorry. That triggered a memory."

We climbed into the car.

She said, "In my job as barmaid I hear many if-only-I-had-the-chance-to-do-it-over stories. It's not often that you get a second chance. Maybe I'll be able to help you with that."

I was thinking, Help me with that? Take a trip to the Speed River where the baby went in and make a marker and bring flowers and set it all up on the shoreline? Is that what she was suggesting? If so, my answer would be no. A firm no. A resolute no. But I could see it coming. Maybe all this Lazore business wasn't about Isabela at all, but about Mario's baby. In the universe of the occult, do drowned babies rise up as adults from the water to haunt you? Is that why I felt I already knew this girl Kirsten? That baby had risen up from the water as Kirsten to lead me to the shore and into the water to leave me there, drowning.

Chapter Eighteen

I had nothing on my calendar for Saturday. I had picked that phrase up from television, "nothing on his calendar." The Lazore was yellow-taped. The police had the nanny. Soon they would find Emily. Nothing on my calendar.

I decided to have lunch at the Deuce. I would sit back with a brew that Kirsten would bring me, and then as I was leaving have a word with her boss about his dress code.

As I parked, I saw two ape-hanger Harleys at the back of the lot. The biker with the chains was there sharing pitchers of beer with a runt biker. From their noise level, I could tell they were already well on their way. The jackets hanging over the chair identified them as the Grimm Reapers. I took a seat two tables over and waited for Kirsten. The tightness of her lips told me she was not happy to see me.

But I noticed that the bikers were happy to see Kirsten, all eyes following her butt working its way in the denim skirt across the room to my table.

"I know, I know, you don't want me here, but I have a question."

"I have a question. Why am I feeling on edge that you're here?" She glanced at the bikers.

I said, loud enough for the bikers to hear, "Tell me who's setting you on edge. I'll have a word with him."

"Don't you dare," she hissed.

I continued, loud enough to be overhead in the parking lot, "Are the bikers setting you on edge with their lustful thoughts?"

"No. Forget it. Leave me alone."

"Any evidence of carnal behaviour from their table?"

"No. Don't order, just leave."

I turned to the one with chains. "You have my permission to look at her, but not with lustful thoughts followed by carnal behaviour."

Kirsten was looking over at the bartender, who was watching the flatscreen and paying no attention.

"I understand, you biker bottom-feeders like to look; she's a looker. I understand that. But the problem is, instead of controlling your lust and keeping it hidden, you're putting it right out on your face where she can see your mind turning thoughts into carnal behaviour, and that puts her on edge."

"I'm thinking I'll call the cops," said Kirsten.

"I'm thinking Chains wants to apologize, to make it easier on himself."

Chains said, "How do you know what I'm thinking?"

"There's a program on TV me and Kirsten watch called *The Dog Whisperer*. He seems to know what the dog is thinking and that's how he trains them to not have lustful thoughts, you know, on people's knees."

"I'm calling the cops," said Kirsten.

"If a dog can be trained which knee to hump and which knee not to hump, then so can a biker."

Kirsten was looking over at the bartender.

"Most bikers aren't as smart as dogs, I know, but I figure with training you can learn to sit in your chairs and behave yourselves when you're in this bar."

A glance at the bartender busy with his beer glasses, pretending he wasn't noticing the storm brewing, suggested he was leaving it to Kirsten to solve the problem.

I said, "Hindsight is a wonderful thing, but foresight is better. Or put it another way: be careful whose knee you decide to hump."

Kirsten said, "If you back off and shut up, I'll bring you a beer."

"I'll have a glass of what the gentlemen at the next table are drinking." I nodded and smiled at the old gentleman with the Guinness.

Kirsten turned away, back to the bar.

"Nice Harleys," I said. "Where you from? Which swamp?"

The bikers did not stare when Kirsten brought me the Guinness. She sat across from me. "I've delivered your beer with a message from Steve, who is about to dial 911. But I won't bring you another because foresight is a wonderful thing and you are definitely humping the wrong knee and you are *definitely* leaving."

I gestured with my beer to Chains. "My apologies. I am mistaken. Where do inner pig-dog lustful thoughts come from? The brain. So, you probably weren't having any — my mistake. You were probably having other thoughts in your brain, about having a shower perhaps, maybe even about laundering your clothes. For example, maybe your brain was saying that if you cleaned yourself up you might get more than just thoughts. Some girl might give you her phone number, but not too many numbers: too hard to remember."

Kirsten got up and returned to the bar. She must have thought Chains was backing off, because she didn't dial the cops, and nor did Steve, who was still busy with his glasses. When Chains waved for another pitcher, she brought it over. As she bent to place it in the centre of the table, Chains's smirking eyes fastened on me as he slid his right hand up between her legs. When she grabbed his arm, she spilled the beer on the tabletop. Both bikers slid their chairs away from the beer dripping on the floor.

Steve came out from behind the bar carrying a rag. He looked like a decent enough guy, like a Jehovah's Witness, in fact, knocking on the front door. But not the front door of a biker house.

"We should get a free pitcher for that," said Chains.

"It was an accident," said Steve. "I'll draw you another one."

"Not an accident," I said. "This scumbag was feeling her up."

Steve looked bewildered.

"I'll show you." I pulled over an empty chair. "Chainman was sitting like this. Kirsten was there. Chainman, stand here so I can show Steve and you get a free pitcher. No hard feelings. I'll pay for it myself."

Sneering, Chains stood next to the chair.

"So Kirsten was here setting down the jug when—" I jammed my hand into Chains's crotch and gave his balls a twisting yank.

"Like that."

Chains bent over coughing as I took out my cell phone. "You want me to phone the cops and press charges, Kirsten? Hello, 911? Someone's on the floor holding his crotch and moaning like he's on an obscene phone call. No cops? What then? You want me to rip off his donkey? Take out his eyes? What do you want me to do?"

She seemed confused and looked to Steve for the answer, who was looking to me for an answer.

I said, "She's just a kid trying to make a living. She needs protection from swamp-dwelling bottom-feeders like these ones you're not protecting her from."

The runt biker said, "She's the wife of that guy who drives for Bob's Towing. You're the one who's going to get his donkey ripped off."

I examined this biker. He looked harmless enough, a tag-along with a beard and bike. He said, "Her husband's name is Billy. He's been looking for her."

I looked at Kirsten for confirmation. When she didn't deny it, I said, "Well, now he's found her and now she's gone. Your shift is over, Kirsten. And so is this job. Let's go."

I took her arm and led her out the door to my car and sat her in the front seat. I started the car and drove to the first light and turned right, watching in my rearview for the Harleys. I made another right and left, but still no bikers.

Kirsten had settled into a sullen pout beside me.

"So now I know. You're on the run from a tow-truck driver called Billy."

She said, "Hindsight is a wonderful thing. You've just humped the wrong knee."

"I'm serious, Kirsten. Every day you check out the window to see who's there. You told the reverend I look after you. You were just giving him a line, I know, but this is where the line ends."

She leveled a glare at me. "How guilty do you feel for making me lose my job?"

"I don't feel guilty at all. If you work in a bar, you need backup."

Kirsten crossed her arms and stared out the window.

"So, I was married."

"Then what?"

"I wasn't married."

"Married for how long?"

"Five years."

"To who?"

"Whom."

"To whom?"

"Billy. He was an independent businessman."

"Good. Okay. A businessman. What kind of business?"

"Bob's Towing."

"I thought his name was Billy."

"It was. Still is."

"Okay. Billy Bob has a tow-truck business. So, what happened?"

"He has a two-truck tow-truck business. Lots of decent men drive tow trucks; some own tow trucks."

Kirsten slid down in her seat and slumped into herself.

"And what did Billy do that you unmarried him?"

"He beat me up once too often."

"So, when did you leave him?"

"The day before I arrived at your house."

"The day you arrived at my house you had no bruises, no black eye."

Now her lower lip was trembling. "They weren't where you could see them."

"So how old were you when you got married? The truth."

"Eighteen."

Kirsten was sniffing back her tears.

"At eighteen, you married a tow-truck driver?"

"So, what of it?"

"They're like bikers with four-strokes between their legs, cavemen with V8s between their legs."

We arrived home. Kirsten went straight upstairs, leaving me thinking about her being married to a tow-truck driver. I had seen it in vice: half the strip clubs were owned by biker clubs, the other half by tow-truck companies. The cops put the tow guys and the biker guys away and told the girls to go home and get their heads on straight.

I felt bad for Kirsten. I wanted to go up and apologize. But first, I needed to give her some fatherly advice. Now I knew her quick wit and smart-ass remarks were defenses against feelings of vulnerability. I was sure of that. Dressing in sexy clothes and adorning herself with bracelets and karmic necklaces was a cover for low self-esteem. I knew that. But it was time Kirsten grew up and moved into the grown-ups' world.

In ten minutes, she returned downstairs dressed in jeans and a sweatshirt.

We sat side by side on the chesterfield.

She said, "About Billy. What was I to do? I called the police tons of times but they never do anything. I had one thought in mind: where can I go that he won't find me? I looked for apartments for rent but the landlords wanted first and last up front. Then I knocked on your door and there you stood. The first thing I thought was, 'He doesn't look mean. In fact, he looks like...' Well, I could tell by your eyes that you were a decent person, and yeah a big bugger, big enough to look after Billy. And then I thought, 'He looks familiar.' And then I remembered seeing you on television when you tried to rescue that baby in the Speed River. And then you agreed to first and last later..."

She went to the window to peek out. "That little biker who came in today — I've never seen him before. Steve knows my new address is your house. Steve is no hero. If Chains wants your address, Steve will give it away. So now, thanks to you, Billy's found me."

"You should know better than to have anything to do with bikers."

"I don't have anything to do with bikers. But my Aunt Bessie rode a bike. That little biker, he must have seen me somewhere with Bessie and Billy."

"Who is Aunt Bessie anyway?"

Kirsten was slow to answer. She looked like she knew this was a loaded question that would lead to others. Despite all those déjà vu hints I had been receiving, I still had no answers. What was the point of having a brain that left memories in storage until, when you needed them, you couldn't remember them, in there still but shriveled up like dried apples, like early-onset Alzheimer's?

Kirsten asked, "You don't remember Aunt Bessie?"

Aunt Bessie? No. But now I remembered a couple of years ago at a cop party when I had noticed Earl, who had taken early retirement, standing alone, looking bewildered. I had gone up to Earl and shook his hand. "How's things, Early?" That's what we called him. Early's face was blank. I could see in his eyes that his mind was desperately trying to remember who I was.

"It's Quinn, from 54 Division."

Parsons told me later, "Early got early retirement because he got early-onset Alzheimer's." Parsons said it with a smile, but I didn't think it was funny then and I especially didn't think it was funny now.

Kirsten's question had been soft, almost a whisper, insignificant compared to the impact of the memory I was now processing: Parsons had worked on the case of the missing girls, but Early had been the lead detective. Early-onset Earl...

Kirsten was waiting. "You don't remember Aunt Bessie?"

"No, I don't remember your Aunt Bessie. Why would I?"

Kirsten sat sullen and pouty, one leg over one knee, her foot rocking. "No. Why should you? It's like your horoscope said, you're a dickhead. That was a warning. But I was willing to give the dickhead a second chance."

"Second? What was the first?"

"It doesn't matter."

She had planted another seed and I could see by the lower lip that she was going to do some high-drama crying with big wet tears to get the seed started.

I left her sniveling on the chesterfield, went into my office bedroom, and shut the door. I opened my laptop to a page on early-onset Alzheimer's.

Chapter Nineteen

The first thing I noticed when I arrived home was that Kirsten was cooking dinner. The second thing was that Kirsten had cleaned up my apartment. Okay, as long as she could remember where she'd put my stuff. I removed my suit jacket and hung it over a chair and sat at the kitchen table.

"Hang it in the closet, please." She was wearing the jean skirt frayed around the bottom, and a T-shirt that bagged around her waist.

I said, "You're looking sullen."

Not wasting a moment, she came back with, "You're looking guilty for making me move."

"Move? Where to?"

She gave me her patented pout. "Oh no, it's not your fault you made me lose my job. So go ahead, rent your stupid apartment to someone with a job who can pay the rent while I go and live in poverty."

"When are you leaving to go and live in poverty?"

"I've already left."

"Then how come you're here?"

"Because I've moved into your apartment."

Sure enough, when I glanced into my spare bedroom/office, I saw all her stuff piled on the floor.

She said, "I moved in here temporarily waiting for the moving company to give me a date."

"Kirsten, can I ask a question?"

"No."

"You only have two suitcases. Why do you need a moving company?"

"Plus all my stuff in my other apartment. The move will cost you about twelve-hundred dollars, two men with a nineteen-wheeler, twelve-hundred dollars plus five-hundred dollars upfront to put my stuff into storage until I find a new place to hide."

She opened the fridge, unsnapped a Corona, and set it in front of me. "You're not a glass person, right? Straight from the neck, right? A macho dude."

She sat beside me on the chesterfield.

"My new temporary job, until I find a new place to hide, is live-in help. I clean your house, cook your dinner, read your mail, go through your stuff, whatever. I'll work for minimum wage. And I want you to pay for the money I spent buying dinner. Meatloaf, mashed potatoes, carrots. Your refrigerator was empty."

"Fourteen dollars an hour for cooking and cleaning?"

"And for my pleasant attitude while I do my live-in housekeeper job."

I was almost afraid to ask the pressing question. "Where are you going to sleep?"

"In the bedroom you're using as an office. So now, with a pleasant attitude, I will serve you your dinner."

"A live-in housekeeper does not wear jean skirts and a baggy T-shirts."

She went into what used to be my office and rifled through a box and disappeared into the bathroom. I drank my beer and opened another. Kirsten returned in a white blouse and blue-and-white sandals.

"Kirsten, you're driving me insane."

"I know I am."

"Do you really have another apartment?"

"None of your business."

She was serving the dinner when a knock sounded on the front door. A glance through the front window at the driverless tow truck parked in front told me it was not the movers.

Kirsten grabbed my arm. "Don't answer it. Maybe he'll go away."

The knock came again. We waited for ten minutes. I could see no one on the street, but the tow truck remained where it was parked. I stepped out and was on my way to the truck when I noticed a man wearing a Wyatt Earp hat, a plaid shirt, blue jeans, and work boots coming from the 7-Eleven on the corner. I waited beside the empty tow truck. The man was already halfway down the block, opening a pack of cigarettes and lighting one up, before he noticed me.

The man knelt to tie the laces of his boot. He adjusted his hat and tucked the tails of his plaid shirt into his jeans. His cigarette flared and the end glowed red as he sucked in the smoke. I couldn't see a face under the brim of the Wyatt Earp, only a dark outline of pale Clint Eastwood shadows.

The man stepped into the road, eased himself into the front seat of the truck, picked up his cell phone, punched in some numbers, and listened.

I said, "So, you're Billy. Pleased to meet you."

Billy tipped back his hat to look at me.

"You need a tow?"

"Hindsight is a wonderful thing, Billy, but foresight is even better. So, in foresight, I'm saying you should now decide that you should not be looking for Kirsten."

Billy's eyes were shaded by his hat, which was stained with grease spots.

"I'm doing you a favour letting you know in advance why you shouldn't be looking for her. That way you'll avoid the hindsight part."

Billy stared at me.

"There's a law against beating up wives. But do like on television: say you're sorry and I'll pass it on and you drive away and I'll forget you were ever here."

Billy said nothing.

"This doesn't look good, Billy, you sitting out here in Bob's tow truck."

Billy laid his cell on the dash.

"You're a tow-truck driver, Billy Bob, so I'm thinking you're not as stupid as your buddies at the Deuce. I'm having trouble understanding why you're not driving away."

Billy Bob's lips were getting tight, so I knew Billy Bob was about to break loose.

"The name's Billy. Just Billy."

"It says here Bob's towing."

Billy leaned to one side, ready to step out, as though he wanted to see what was written on his truck.

"That's right, Billy. Bob's Towing. You're right. No need to get out and check. But there's nothing here that needs towing. Except you, if you don't leave."

Billy started his truck.

"Here's a little more advice. Get rid of the hat. It makes you look like a cupcake."

Billy drove away.

"He doesn't say much," I said to Kirsten, who had been watching out the window. "What's with the hat?"

"His birthday is September 17, the same as Billy the Kid. I bought it for him at a flea market. He's not that bad a guy, a softy at heart, he looks after his dad."

"Yeah, right. Cry me a river. And helps old ladies across the street."

I followed her into the dining room.

"I told him he looked like a cupcake."

Her dish-out spoon was suspended halfway between the dish and the plate. "That's like poking a bear with a stick." She began to serve the potatoes. "I can't believe it. You called him a cupcake. You intentionally pick fights. You have an anger-management problem. You need to get therapy."

I took my place at the table. I noted she had set it with extra care, napkins on the right in round holder things I did not know I had. In the centre were candles in proper candlesticks that she must have found by snooping through my stuff. She must have a dessert coming up, because she'd placed a separate spoon above the plates.

She lit the candle, turned off the lights, and sat down opposite me, and after a while I figured it out. "What is this, the Last Supper?"

"I didn't mean it that way, but yes. This was in your cards. I saw it, but I didn't want to believe it. Your days in paradise are numbered, dude. First Chains, now Billy. Eat your dinner while you still can. They're both on the way with their buddies to trash you and your house and me along with it."

I said, "Kirsten. Can I ask you a question?"

"Don't bother."

"Something I don't understand about you being married to a tow-truck driver; nothing against tow-truck drivers, except that they're into insurance fraud and strip clubs and narcotics. But you're a classy person. The match doesn't fit."

"Is there a question on the horizon?"

"How could someone as smart as you—"

She interrupted, "Can you write in your last will and testament that I can still live here after your funeral? I won't have you cremated even if you're counting on it being your last attempt at a smoking hot body. Besides, I don't want your ashes sitting on the mantlepiece. That's the stupidest thing I ever heard of."

"I don't have a mantlepiece. Normal people spread them in the garden."

"You don't have a garden."

I sighed. "I give up. What's the use? Fetch me another beer."

She brought me the beer and went back to her dinner. "It's not what you think. Tow-truck drivers have wives, mothers, grandmothers."

"So, what's your point?"

"What's my point? I'll tell you what's my point. Try to keep up. If you were driving along and you saw someone stuck on the roadside, you would know right away what the situation was. You would read the situation, like Billy and his tow truck: he sees what the situation needs and he temporarily parks his truck and he takes out his jumper cables and he gets the people back on the road with a boost or a charge or whatever. When I arrived at your doorstep, I saw right away that you were stuck in the ditch and your battery was flat and you needed a boost to get back on the road. So how was I going to do that? I'm not a doctor. I have no pills. So, I took a lesson from Billy. I temporarily parked my truck and I used my jumper cables to charge your battery and give you a boost to get you back on the road. And now, after me doing all that for you, you're throwing me out. Well, thanks a lot."

She got up and peeked out the window and came back and sat down. I did not look at her. I didn't know what she was thinking, but I figured she was waiting for me to say that she could stay, which I might have if I'd been looking at her.

I said, "That story sounds like that other pointless story about the execution. It had no meaning that I could figure out, but I'm looking forward all the same to you telling me the meaning of this pointless yarn."

Kirsten went back to her sullen chewing, her fork held properly, thumb and finger like the Queen.

I laid down my fork. "Kirsten. It feels like things are getting dark in here. It feels like I need the lights turned on so I can see what you look like."

She turned on the lights. She was looking weepy.

I said, "I'm sorry. I've ruined the dinner that you spent a lot of time to make. I apologize."

Kirsten said, "That wasn't a pointless story. But if that's what you think of me, I'm leaving. I'm going to stay in a hotel."

"You don't have another apartment?"

"No."

"Well, you can't leave. For the time being, since you've moved down here already, you sleep in the spare bedroom or on the couch, but I can't let you leave."

"Why the change of mind?"

I finished my beer. "Kirsten, can I tell you a pointless story?"

"Try me."

"One evening, a few days before you arrived on my doorstep, the doorbell rang. I paid the pizza guy. It looked good, five different toppings, and smelled delicious. I sat down at the dining room table with my beer, like I am now. But I was afraid to settle in and enjoy the pizza for two reasons. One, because there was too much of everything. I couldn't figure out what I was looking at. And two, because I couldn't remember ever making any connection with a pizza place. I didn't remember ordering it. So now, number one, when I look at you I can't figure out what I'm looking at because there's too much of everything, and two, since I've never had any connection with Billy or Aunt Bessie, I can't figure out where you came from. The thing is, after the mention of Alzheimer's, I'm starting to wonder if I've got it."

"OhmygoshohmyGod! Dude! Fling back the friggin' night! You mean all this time while you're trying to figure out who I am you've been thinking you've got Alzheimer's?"

"I found out later it was Parsons who sent me the pizza."

"No, dude, you do not have Alzheimer's. But the one thing you need to pay attention to right now is, next time your doorbell rings it won't be the pizza that you don't remember ordering."

Her weepy act gone, she smiled. "Well, it was a good story all the same and I realize that these last few weeks have been a tiresome effort for you."

I asked the question: "So who are you?"

"You mentioned a dream. Let's look at that again, the bucket perched on the edge of the stone well with a large iron crank. From the rattle of the bucket and the grating of the crank and the blackness of the well, the child becomes frightened and begins to scream, her high, thin voice shrilling up from the darkness as the bucket disappears down the hole. In desperation, you grab the rope, not bothering with the crank, and in the bucket, up comes ... surprise ... me."

I closed my eyes. I counted to ten. I said, "Get me another beer."

Chapter Twenty

I heard them first and went to the window: four unbaffled Harleys. Kirsten said, "You stay out of it, mind your own business, take a hike, let me handle it."

But I followed her part way down the sidewalk. The bikers stayed on their bikes. Chains said to Kirsten, "Billy don't like your boyfriend and neither do I."

"He's not my boyfriend. He's my father."

Chain scoffed. "Prove it."

Kirsten opened her purse and gave Chains a letter. "This is from my lawyer explaining how an adult child, that would be me, can sue the absent father, that would be him. The first thing is to get the DNA test." She held up an official paper. "You probably can't read the big words, but it's a court-recognized DNA report."

Chains tried to take the papers but she held them back. "Your hands are dirty. It's not that easy to get a good match. How do you collect someone's spit without them knowing it? You move in with them until you get some good spit. So. If you put him in the hospital, he won't be able to work, and if he can't work, he can't pay me back the child support he would have owed my mother."

Chains looked like he was trying to figure this out. "Then you'll go back with Billy?"

"That's up to my father." She pointed my way. "He's Detective Quinn, a vice cop from 54 Division. He knows how harassment and stalking and domestic abuse works, and he knows about bikers and drugs and strip clubs, and so do his buddies in vice, so no, he doesn't want me to go back with Billy. But he does want to pay me the money he owes. Who knows, maybe Billy can sue me for half."

The biker standing next to Chains said. "I know Quinn. You don't fuck with Quinn, man."

Kirsten returned the letters to her purse. The bikers left, Chains in the lead, the other three following. As they disappeared around the corner Kirsten said, "See? No fights. Easy peasy. No need to raise your leg."

Prepared to finally meet Aunt Bessie, I held out my hand for the papers. She gave them to me. I studied both pages. "This is your application for Criminology at Humber College. And this one is just a report confirming you don't have a criminal record."

Kirsten shrugged. "It's like I planted a seed."

Chapter Twenty-One

I liked this live-in arrangement: the housekeeper sleeping in what used to be my spare bedroom/office; the housekeeper getting up early to make me coffee and breakfast; the housekeeper having my dinner in the oven, a bottle of wine and two glasses on the table. Added to that, the housekeeper, instead of high heels and shorts or leggings and almost anything on top, wore decently modest blouses and white capris. And bare feet. I wasn't sure how the bare feet fit into this picture.

I had not had time to advertise the apartment. I was getting lots of calls from the cheated. The yellow tape meant the Lazore was still out of bounds. The police were still looking for Emily. And so far, no sign of Billy or Chains. But the fact that Kirsten had not mentioned the Lazore told me she was still afraid to leave the house because of them and was leaving the investigation to the police. I would have been okay with that. Except for the fact I had remembered the Early story.

Kirsten was standing in the kitchen doorway, having just finished doing the dishes. I was sitting on the chesterfield typing my reports and watching the news. She said, "My fingers are long and slender; yours are too big for your laptop. Instead of hiding out in your apartment all day, I could sit at your desk in your office and say "Quinn and Associates" into the telephone and take down the particulars and make appointments at the same time as I'm typing your cheater reports. By the way, what happened to the professor lady and the horny student?"

"Her and the husband are trying to work it out."

"You see? Anything *I* type will be grammatically correct."

I handed her a cheque made out to Quinn and Associates. She made a fake gasp. "What did this person get for this five thousand dollars? In other words, what did you do to earn it?"

"Where's my beer?"

She brought a Corona. The lime on the rim was a nice barmaid's touch. She sat across from me.

"Here's the story. Anna, age 26, and husband Ronnie, age 29, and neighbour Jack, age 30, and wife Sharon, age 24. Jack was riding Ronnie's exercise bike while he, Ronnie, was away at work. Jack was coming home all sweaty, which was okay, but Jack's wife, Sharon, became suspicious about the riding. She knew Anna wasn't taking birth control and was allergic to latex so she didn't think Anna would be doing any fooling around. But the sweat on Jack when he came home from the riding had an aroma of Anna. Sharon decided to have it checked out. So, first thing after Ronnie drove off to work, and Jack went over to do his riding. Sharon phoned me, Detective Quinn who came and took the pictures."

"Why didn't she do the deed herself? I mean, like, take her own pictures."

"She said confrontation went against who she was. Here's where human nature kicked in. Jack had been confiding in Anna, and had blamed his infidelity on his wife because the marriage had been coming apart. Not Jack's fault, no, of course not. And Ronnie wanted to keep Anna and didn't want to lose his best buddy Jack, no, of course not. But to be able to do that he had to forgive Anna and Jack, but to do that he needed to blame someone, namely me. They said if I hadn't got mixed up in it and turned it sleazy, they would have solved it themselves. We all make mistakes and forgiveness was in order and cry me a river."

"So dude, what you're saying is, if I had been involved, with my amazing social skills, which you're lacking, like empathy..."

"What's empathy got to do with it?"

"The way you told the story, it's all just a big joke to you. That's why they were able to blame you, like you were enjoying yourself at their expense."

"I doubt it. Ronnie wouldn't let it go. We met in a coffee shop. I told him to consider himself lucky. The cheaters weren't wearing protection. He almost ended up raising Jack's kid. That's when Ronnie tried to punch me out."

"And what did you do?"

"Nothing. He missed."

"Then what?"

"I called him a cupcake."

Kirsten gave me her look. "Dude. Let's pause for a moment's reflection." She held up both bare feet. "See this crooked toe?"

I examined the big toe that was a little crooked.

"The reason I've been going barefoot is that this toe is bent. It has trouble getting along with the other toes when it's confined in a tight space, like in a shoe. The reason I sometimes wear big clunky shoes is to give this toe more room. But I don't go barefoot outside because it's not proper. I follow the rules of civilized behaviour."

"I get the feeling there's going to be a message in this story."

"What happened, dude, is this. Try to keep up. Rather than leave the relationship and go out on his own and start again and find someone new that he might be able to trust, it's easier for Ronnie to pretend the problem got solved. The anger is still there waiting to get triggered, which is what you did when you called him a cupcake. It was totally unnecessary."

She disappeared into the spare bedroom and sorted through her stuff and brought back a small package for me to open. "There are two good reasons you need me: the first is to teach you about empathy. The capacity for empathy is inherited; how and when to use it is learned. With all those years as a vice cop you've lost your capacity for empathy and replaced it with rules and procedures and cynicism. You've wrapped yourself in yellow tape. The yellow tape is like your tie, hanging down, getting in the way, ending up in your double-double. This is a classic tie bar in sterling silver. It's engraved."

I read it out loud. "'Always.' What does that mean?"

"It means you'll always mess up because you're a bent toe. But if I'm always working for you, I can help you in two ways. I can help you fit in with the other toes and I can help you keep your yellow tape clipped to your shirt instead of hanging down and getting in the way."

I shifted my laptop so she could fasten the clip to my tie. She sat next to me and gave me a reproachful look. She crossed her arms and stared at me with sad eyes. "I lied. The tie clip is an apology gift. I will always and forever be sorry for the fact that I used you for my own protection."

"But..." She hoisted her bare foot onto my knee. "Let's not get carried away with remorse. Have a good look at the toe. If you stop acting like a bent toe and stop insulting people and picking fights, I will work, not *for* you, no way, but *with* you at your detective agency. But I have to tell you, right now, you're a disappointment to me for not looking for Emily. So I've been all by myself, risking my life. I've been crossing that stupid yellow tape. Do you know why? Because if the cops had done a thorough search of the Lazore, they would have found our fingerprints. Your fingerprints must be on file. Why haven't they come knocking at your door? Because they didn't do a thorough search."

Chapter Twenty-Two

I ducked under the yellow tape and followed her up the front walk and through the weeds of the side yard to the back door of the Lazore. She said, "I opened the hurricane doors into the basement. There's something not right down there, even excepting the fact that it's full of rats. I got a feeling like I was standing in an empty attic with no light, waiting. Except I was in the basement."

I had never been waiting in an attic or a basement. I said, "So, I'll get you a flashlight."

"It's not about needing a flashlight. It's got nothing to do with a flashlight. I don't need a flashlight to know Isabela is down there. If I stand in the attic, I know she's not there. If I stand in the living room, I know she's not there. If I stand in the basement, I know she's there. The feeling is like the one I get when I stand on the veranda. Mrs. Lazore is there with their suitcases, waiting while Dr. Lazore buries Isabela in the basement. If I go into the basement, Isabela is there waiting to be brought up and strapped into her booster seat. I can feel it. So why if I can feel Isabela and Mrs. Lazore are here, why can't I feel that Emily is here? Because she's in Lois's basement."

Kirsten opened the back door. I followed her into the living room. I said, "How am I supposed to make sense of what you just said?"

"Jesus, dude. If you don't start paying attention, I'm going to kill you."

"Well, go ahead and kill me, but hurry back because I want to know why you think Emily is in Lois's basement."

"Look around. The furniture is sitting here waiting for the Lazore family to come back, the pictures are hanging here waiting, the statue of Gabriella is standing out there waiting. Time has stopped. The Lazore is waiting for that baby to rise up from under the concrete so life can go on."

I sighed. "What's that got to do with Emily being in Lois's basement?"

"Lois is Gabriella. She's keeping Emily, aka Isabela, in her basement until she can bring her over here and bury her with the other Isabelas."

"Why not in the Lazore basement?"

"The real Isabela is in that basement and that's where she would like them all to be, except she would need a jack hammer for every Isabela. So she puts the other Isabelas out here so their big sister can keep an eye on them."

She was right. Of course.

She sighed. "Finally. I was beginning to think you should be the one sitting behind the desk making the appointments. So, here's what's next: number one, we get my dress from Lois, which should be ready by now. While we're there we figure out a way to get back into her house so we can do a thorough search."

Kirsten sat on the chesterfield. She crossed one leg over the other. She held her hands in her lap. "Dude. Listen to Kirsten. The I Ching says, 'Not many words spoken, not many statements made, but an invisible thread every so often joins the shadows of one person to the shadow of the other and they connect.' That is what we're doing, following the invisible thread joining Lois to the three little girls to Isabela to Emily."

"Okay, the sewing. I'm okay with that. But breaking into Lois's house? No, we can't do that. I'll lose my license. Better to phone Parsons."

Her eyes flashed anger. "Dude! Get with it. Parsons is part of the problem. Yellow-tape thinking. What's more important, Emily, or your license?"

Kirsten returned to the kitchen window. She called me over and pointed. I watched Lois shut the back door and step down her back stoop. In one hand she was carrying what looked like a shoebox, and in the other, a shovel. She entered the Lazore yard through the hole in the fence, crossed through the weeds, and disappeared along the side of the house. From the front window, we watched her dig a hole next to the statue. She set the shovel aside and gently placed the box into the hole. By now it was too dark to see exactly what she was doing until, when the street lights blinked on, I saw her take from her coat pocket a doll with a white collar and black suit, like a priest. She knelt by the hole and held the doll priest at the edge and she said some words. Then with her fingers, she held up the arms of the priest and threw in a handful of dirt. She set the priest aside. She patted the sod back into place to hide the hole. She and the priest knelt at its feet and said a prayer.

Lois returned to her kitchen.

I followed Kirsten to the front walk and from there to the statue. She said, "I can't understand why no one would pay attention to what Lois was doing here in this side yard. Surely someone passing would notice." She glanced around. "But maybe not. Thick shadows and no lighted windows meant Lois could stay well hidden."

I knew what was coming next.

"If Lois can dig and not get caught, so can Kirsten."

Chapter Twenty-Three

First thing next morning was Home Depot.

"Dude, it's obvious to me that you've never been in a Home Depot. We come through the doors and you stand there looking like a man in ladieswear. The shovels will be in the gardening department, straight ahead."

I followed her. I began to check out the shovels.

"Just between us girls, dude, that's a square-mouthed gravel shovel. And that's a snow shovel." She selected one with a round mouth and short handle.

Then I didn't know how to work the self-checkout, which was the only way to pay.

She said, "Here's the plan. The Lazore is falling into ruin. As a neighbour, I want to do something about this unacceptable situation. First off, I want to clean up the yard. I want to plant daffodils around the statue, or tulips, whatever comes up every spring. I want to cut back the weeds and trim the hedges and—"

"And first off, what happens when the police come by and start asking questions about your crossing the yellow tape? And second off, Lois can see you from her kitchen window."

"First off, the police aren't interested in the Lazore: we can take down the tape and they'll never notice. And second off, Lois can't see us from her kitchen window. I already checked. So, stop giving me a hard time. Either help me, or I'll see you later. Make your own supper and fetch your own beer."

I parked a few doors down from the Lazore, got the shovel out of the trunk, and stood waiting for instructions while Kirsten rambled on about a flower garden around the historic statue of

Gabriella, like in Ottawa with all those historic statues of Champlain and Macdonald and those other murderers of children.

Kirsten searched through the grass by the statue, digging here and there at random, it seemed. "Why don't you dig up the shoebox?"

She said, "Lois has replaced the sod so I can't tell where anything might be buried."

Kirsten continued to dig at the base of the statue.

"There are no worms."

She continued to dig.

"There should be worms."

She was on her hands and knees now, poking into the freshly turned sod. She looked like a seven-year-old kid playing in the mud, hands getting dirty, legs covered with muck.

"I saw the Garden of Eden in my Tarot cards. They were saying something about the flowers and the sun." Kirsten glanced around. She looked at the sky. She looked at the trees. "I'm trying to figure out about the sun. I've never thought about the sun as a symbol like the I Ching bones. But look, there it is, peeking at us over a treetop one block over, across the street from Lois's house. The stars and the planets are up there, receiving directions from the sun. The whole galaxy is receiving its direction from the sun. And now here I am, receiving my directions from the sun. It is right now lining me up with the cosmic influences hidden by the daytime sky like bones in the grass directing me to the exact spot marked by taking a certain number of paces in a certain direction away from the statue to where the flies gather."

She hesitated. "But there are no flies today."

I said, "Lois is getting old. What's she going to do when she can't dig anymore?"

Kirsten flopped over on her back in the grass and closed her eyes. With a sigh she said, "How is poor Mr. Quinn doing? Oh, he's doing his best, muddling along. He's on the list for the home but, you know, the list is a mile long. Jesus help me, it's not about getting rid of bodies, dude. Yellow-tape thinking. The police will never find them, especially now they've got two nannies with foreign names to blame, racist pigs."

She began to kick through the weeds, muttering about why no flies, following what looked like either a shadow or a sunken depression leading from the statue to the Lazore's stone foundations. Now the sun was above the trees. She glanced around. "Here is direct sun. Why are there no flies? Why are there no sunken depressions? Direct sun would dry the earth faster, the grave dirt would sink deeper, the bodies decompose quicker. There should be depressions."

She returned to the statue and stood by the freshly dug earth. "This is not working. Needle in a graveyard. Let's check inside."

I followed her into the Lazore. She went into the office room and stood looking out the window, organizing her thoughts, calculating the correlations of planetary positions to determine where to sink her shovel, at least that's what it looked like.

"My digging idea isn't working." She stood at the back door, looking out. "The fact that she hasn't started digging yet means Emily is still alive. Will you give me money to buy night-vision binoculars so that I can stay here all night and watch Lady Lois digging her next grave or cleaning the statue or whatever she's going to do next?"

There was no point in telling her she couldn't stay all night. I left her at the Lazore and drove to the mall to buy the binoculars. We took turns at three-hour watches. At each trade-off Kirsten stretched out on the couch and fell asleep. I didn't fit on the couch, so I sat in the doctor's high-backed chair and thought about the all-night stakeouts in my past. Here I was doing exactly the same thing that I had retired from. At dawn, with no sign of Lois, we left.

Chapter Twenty-Four

Kirsten came from the bathroom, ready to pick up her altered dress. I wasn't sure how the sunglasses perched on top of her head, their arms buried in her side-saddle braid, looking very Miami Beach, her outfit complete with frayed cut-offs and a spaghetti-strap top, fit in with picking up an altered dress from Lois, the child-killer. Or the sandals, for that matter. "I thought your crooked toe was an embarrassment."

Kirsten looked at her feet. "Do you want to know how it got crooked? I'll tell you. When I was sixteen I was at a bush party and I slammed it against a rock in the dark. The reason it's crooked is that I didn't tell Aunt Bessie because she had told me I couldn't go to the bush party. So my guilt caused it to heal crooked."

I parked the car across the street from Lois's house. Kirsten said, "I'm getting bad feelings in my toe about that upside-down crucifix knocker guilt thing on her front door."

I said, "Maybe that knocker was there when Lois bought the house. There's a Greek Orthodox Church around the corner. They probably give upside-down door knockers for first communion or baptism or whatever."

"No church gives out upside-down door knockers. How could an upside-down door knocker work anyway? The door would need to be upside down. Then the numbers would be upside down."

I knocked with the crucifix knocker and we waited.

I tested the door. "No answer, and the door is locked." I returned to the sidewalk to get a more thorough look at the house, obviously owned by a single woman with no husband: the eaves filled with debris, seedlings growing in the muck, the downspouts missing.

The alley between Lois's house and Emily's next door was overgrown with weeds, as was the small backyard. I climbed the steps of the back stoop and knocked again, cupping my hand to peer into a small kitchen. I circled the house, picking my way through the weeds to a second basement window. I cupped my hands against the glass, but this window was covered with plywood from the inside. I returned to the front, climbed the steps of the porch, and again pressed cupped hands against the glass of the front window. Nothing unusual, except for a block of wood holding the front window open an inch.

Kirsten stood on the front walk, looking at me over her sunglasses that were halfway down her nose. She said, "Anyone wanting to break in could simply raise the window and crawl through."

"Looks like it."

"My sewing is in there, ready for pickup."

"We'll have to come back." I said this sternly, knowing she was already plotting a plan in her busy head.

Sure enough, after a glance up and down the street, Kirsten raised the window, climbed inside, released the lock of the front door, climbed out the window, and tried the door.

She stepped back. "Looks suspicious, dude, an unlocked door on the home of an elderly lady in the downtown of a big city. I think you should investigate."

"No can do. That's breaking and entering."

"But I came to pick up my sewing, saw a Satanic symbol on the front door, found the door unlocked, wide open in fact, so understandably, I couldn't just walk away."

"No way, Kirsten..."

"Reverend Beachy asked us to keep an eye on her."

Wanting nothing to do with this, I walked away. I wandered around to the back and stood at the fence looking into the backyard of the Lazore. From this position, I could see that the knee-high weeds of the yard were well tramped into a bare path from Lois's fence to the statue. Kirsten would say that the path of Lois's daily pilgrimage, like serial-killer notes to the police giving them clues, was her way of saying, Please catch me, I'm tired of washing my hands.

My cell phone rang.

Kirsten's voice said, "I'm here at Lois Miller's to pick up my sewing and there was no answer but the front door was unlocked and wide open and then I noticed a Satanic knocker on the door and remembered the reverend said she might be suffering from weirdness and I promised him I would check on her, so I'm stepping in to check it out."

"You are not stepping in to check it out."

"Oh-oh, my foot with the crooked toe is now preceding me through the doorway and oh-oh, too late, my foot is following the crooked toe into the kitchen."

I hung up and hurried to the front of the house. Kirsten came down from upstairs. "There's a large master bedroom and two smaller ones but her sewing machine is in the kitchen. And where are the dolls?"

Kirsten sat on the couch and crossed her bare legs. "She's got two spare bedrooms upstairs, so why isn't one for sewing? Seamstresses always have a sewing room. Where is it?"

I handed her an envelope I had just found on the kitchen table. Inside were several three-by-five pictures, all of rag dolls lined up in a row on some sort of workbench. Off to one side stood a sewing machine.

Kirsten said, "So where is this room?"

She examined the pictures one by one. "This one looks like the priest, and this one is an undertaker. What is that telling you?"

"That we should get out of here before she comes home."

Kirsten moved a little closer so I could see where she was pointing. "This one looks sort of ghoulish, like a second undertaker. And this T-shirt on this little girl doll, see the emblem across the front? It looks like a picture of the Gabriella statue made of embroidered sequins."

She shifted against me on the couch, her arm and shoulder against mine as she pointed. "Look at them. Hint, hint. Think Lady Macbeth."

"Hint hint yourself. We have to get out of here before she comes home."

I returned the pictures to the envelope and returned the envelope to the kitchen table. Kirsten followed me along the hallway to the front door where she abruptly stopped. "We didn't check that door off the kitchen."

The door opened onto unpainted wooden steps into a finished basement room containing a washer, dryer, furnace, and water heater.

"There's no door off this room," said Kirsten. "But it is smaller than the main floor."

"The rest is probably crawl-space."

"Where is the sewing room?"

I heard the rattle of the keys in the front-door lock.

No time to waste, I took her arm and we climbed the stairs, opened the back door, and hurried across the yard to the fence, which Kirsten vaulted in one leap. Too big to go through the missing board gap, I heaved and climbed and grunted and dropped with a plunk into the Lazore yard. Coming up on hands and knees, I peered into what looked like a groundhog hole.

Kirsten crouched beside me. "Told you."

I said, "Never mind that now. When she comes into the kitchen, she'll see you left the basement door ajar, and if she looks out her window, she'll see me, the person who broke into her house, on his hands and knees in the weeds."

We hurried to the car. As I pulled away from the curb, Kirsten said, "Right now, there should be a police cruiser on its way to answer a break-in call. Unless she's got something to hide."

I circled the block and parked two doors down from Lois's house. We waited.

"Groundhog hole," said Kirsten, staring at the back of the Lazore. "They burrow down and tunnel underground and dig another opening. They always have a front and back door."

"Maybe," I said.

Kirsten sighed. "That's what you always say, maybe."

"So?"

"There you go again. I'm a stupid blonde barmaid so I don't know anything."

"You're not a blonde. Groundhogs don't live in the city." I checked my rearview mirror. No police car.

Kirsten sighed a big one. "Try to keep up, dude." She unfastened her sunglasses from her hair and fastened them over her eyes. "The hardest part about being a barmaid is trying to figure out who is drunk and who is stupid. I know you're not drunk. Of course they don't live in the city. But fifty years ago they did, and they didn't backfill their holes when they left."

Kirsten sat quietly, her sunglasses perched on her nose.

I said, "How far in school did this smart barmaid get?"

"I went to college and became a specialist barmaid."

"I think if you want to become a detective, you need some formal education. Did you graduate from high school, Kirsten?"

"Of course I did. You have to work really hard to not graduate from high school, like be in a coma."

"So, after high school, you married Billy Bob?"

She was staring into her sideview mirror, either checking for the police or thinking up a smart answer. She said, "Yeah, and then I ran away from Billy Bob, so now I'm broke, unemployed, and so destitute that I would've been living on the street but for the fact that you hired me to be your housekeeper, which is a demeaning job for a detective associate. That's why I want my name on the company business card. Detective, not housekeeper."

Her hands were clasped in the lap of her cut-offs, her thumb running back and forth against the palm of her hand, a sign she was sorting through her thoughts. I *tap-tapped* the finger of my right hand against her left arm. "The police aren't coming."

I started the car. But when I checked the mirror before pulling away from the curb, I saw the tow truck pull up behind me. I climbed out of the car. Kirsten opened her door and came around to the driver's side to stand beside me.

Billy wasn't wearing his hat but he otherwise looked the same as last time with blue jeans and a Bob's Towing T-shirt. He said, "I want Kirsten to take a ride with me."

"He wants me to take a ride with him," said Kirsten.

"Do you want to take a ride with him?"

"No, I don't."

"Well then, tell him."

"He says to tell you I don't want to take a ride with you."

Billy was five inches shorter than me but was powerfully built, Italian-looking with curly black hair.

"This is my father," said Kirsten, sliding her sunglasses into her hair. "I've moved in with him and moved on. It's time for you to move on. We can get divorce papers at Staples. We both sign on the bottom line and it's a done deal, all she wrote."

"Do I get half the child support he owes you?"

I stepped in. "Of course. A happy occasion," I said. "Father and son-in-law." I picked up Billy's hanging arm and shook Billy's short-fingered hand.

"Over the moon," said Kirsten. "Give Billy a hug."

"This is the hand of someone who does heavy work," I said.

"I hated those hands. They felt like sandpaper."

"Maybe from the battery acid," I said. "It eats away the skin."

"Some girls like rough hands, for some weird reason," said Kirsten.

"My advice, Billy: before you put up your dating profile on the internet, get some cream for your hands."

"Maybe not," said Kirsten. "When he fills in the section for his special skills, he can say he gives back rubs and back scratches at the same time."

"Don't be a smart-ass, Kirsten." And then to Billy, I said, "Hindsight is a wonderful thing. But foresight is better. Trust me. You're better off without her."

She pointed at me. "And you're better off without him. He's sometimes short of manners."

"Let's just say, Billy, we are assisting you in redirecting your life."

"What about the money?"

"Uhh ... I wouldn't count on it."

We left Billy standing by his tow truck.

"Billy doesn't seem too smart," I said as we climbed into the car.

She smiled as she buckled herself in. "That's why I liked him. He made me feel intelligent and superior, which is a low self-esteem thing; I guess that comes from not having a dad."

She settled herself next to me. She seemed to be waiting for an answer to her last comment. Finally, she asked, "Did you ever think of having kids, Quinn?"

She never called me just Quinn. When I looked at her closely, I saw in her eyes her anticipation of that baby rising up from the concrete in the Lazore, and of another baby rising up from muddy water here, now.

"No, I did not."

"Maybe you have one you don't know about."

"Not possible," I said.

"How do you know?"

"I had a football accident that rendered me useless."

"When were you tested?"

"I don't remember. Around 1998."

"Tests weren't reliable in 1998."

"Maybe it wasn't 1998. Why are you asking?"

Kirsten hesitated, too long. "I don't know, seeing those pictures of rag dolls, thinking about when I was a little girl, how I had no mother and no father and no friends except my rag dolls."

For me, the sentence did not end. It trailed off, or more like floated off, to snag itself, like so many other things about Kirsten, somewhere along the muddy shoreline of my mind.

Chapter Twenty-Five

We drove home. I followed Kirsten into the house and into the living room, where we sat side by side on the chesterfield. I turned on the Ducks which seemed to be on 24/7. This episode was about how, deep down inside his hip waders, Willie wasn't into duck calls anymore, especially now that they were changing the call to a higher frequency which could call ducks from farther away but could damage the hearing of ducks close by.

At the commercial break, Kirsten said, "I have good hearing because of the shape of my ear. Look at it."

"I've already looked at your ear."

"The ear pattern is like an S for better hearing,"

I studied the pattern of her ear. "It looks like an anchor, like at Sailor's."

"An ear can't look like an anchor."

"Good for anchoring those dangly earrings."

She took my finger and traced the pattern. "See how it sort of cups out to catch the faintest sound? While we were standing in Lois's basement, I could hear a faint sound on the other side of that wall."

"All I heard was the rattle of keys in the lock."

"I've been thinking about that groundhog hole. As you said, groundhogs don't live in the city, at least not anymore, not downtown. Rats don't usually go underground into tunnels. But that groundhog tunnel is still being used by something; otherwise, it would have filled in."

"Meaning?"

"Remember that first day I looked at the statue? I noticed botflies swarming around. Rats chew on bones, like dogs, to sharpen their teeth. And the minerals are part of their diet."

"Meaning?"

"The groundhog hole tunnels into a grave near the statue. The rats found a body buried down there. That explains the flies, and if you say 'Meaning?' I'm going to kill you."

"Well, go ahead, but hurry back because the commercial is over."

Watching the Ducks was a total waste of one of God's good fruits, namely intelligence, but if Kirsten liked it, I wanted to like it. Except she wasn't watching it. She was slumped against me, staring with a pensive expression at her toe.

She said, "Remember my Aunt Bessie? You don't. But anyway, Bessie had a pet rat. She had a little harness and would take him for walks and he'd answer to his name which was Mr. Bojangles because he liked to take her car keys out of her purse and make them jingle. Other things too. He'd take out her lipstick; she wore this heavy red stuff she smeared on, or her pen or whatever, and bring them to her. When he wanted to go for a walk, he'd bring her his harness but not in the day because they're nocturnal. So, at night the rats go poking around the graves and find little-girl bones. I bet if I did a thorough search of the Lazore basement, which is full of rats, I'd find little-girl bones."

A neighbour of the Ducks had stolen the woodchipper, thinking he could plant the chips and grow trees. The Ducks explained to the neighbour that he could not grow trees from woodchips, but that they would be glad to show him how to plant seeds.

I knew that Kirsten was intentionally planting the name Bessie in my mind, and every mention of it was water on the seed of the Speed River baby she was trying to grow, into what I did not know. So, when the Ducks went to commercials, which seemed to be every five minutes, I asked, "Kirsten, I sometimes get this feeling that you are drawing me some sort of self-serving map. You're filling it in one street at a time, one turn at a time. But I'm not getting it. It's like trying to fly backward. Helicopters can fly backward, even sideways. But we aren't in a helicopter. If you're trying to take me somewhere, stop trying to take me backward."

She shifted the sunglasses from the top of her head to the end of her nose to stare at me over the top of the frame.

"If you're thinking everything I have done so far is self-serving, you're right. But we're not there yet. I'm moving forward the only way I know how. I know for you it must be like always listening but being too far away to hear. Memories can travel both backward and forward, but they can never stop traveling."

Chapter Twenty-Six

As far as I was concerned, Kirsten, her Night Owls slung around her neck and a high-powered flashlight in her right hand, looked suspicious enough for a neighbour to phone the police. I made sure I parked well away from the property, that my flashlight was concealed, and I walked several paces behind her, pretending that I wasn't with her.

I placed a chair at the Lazore kitchen window opposite Lois's kitchen window. To focus the Night Owls, I slid them along the backyard of Emily's house. There were two upstairs windows with brown trim in the red-brick wall. Downstairs was one kitchen window and one back door, leading out to a small back stoop with three wooden steps to the yard. I drifted along Lois's backyard and then zoomed up the back wall. When I focused on the end-to-end squares of brick, I could see that Lois's house needed repairs along the eaves where, one by one, the bats were coming out to begin their early evening hunt, swooping across the yard to catch the botflies that would be circling in the light falling from the street lights above the statue. I glided down to her stone foundation and noted it had cracks big enough to let rats come in and out.

I shifted over to the back of the house next door, where a man silently painted the inside frame of his kitchen window pale yellow to match the walls. I skated back to Emily's house. Her mother was eating a late supper, her mouth silently chewing, her head bowed. Not a happy picture.

I coasted across the backyards of the three houses, then zoomed into Lois's kitchen window. It was like pulling the table and chairs, fridge, and stove through the glass; the binoculars set the kitchen down right in front of me. My focus came to rest on Lois standing at the sink, her face scowling, her mousy hair pulled back in a bun. She looked like she had stepped out of one of Dr. Lazore's family photos. I felt like I was looking through the picture glass of a framed portrait of the adult Gabriella. It was like I was following a thread backward in time. This was the sixth-sense feeling Kirsten had gradually been giving me, not like handing it to me or taking me to it, but like catching it from her like a virus. She had the gift. She could fly with it, backward or sideways or forward, but it left me hovering, for how much longer I did not know.

At the window facing the side yard, I swept my focus through the weeds to the side view of the statue. My fingers brought the statue into the room to stand in front of me, so clear I could see the pout of its lower lip that Kirsten had seen a few days into our investigation.

Back to Lois. Her stoop light came on and she stepped out. Now her plastered-down hair and thin, scowling face made her look like she'd just come in out of the rain. But I knew this wasn't true, for my binoculars were so powerful I could see there were no raindrops anywhere I focused. That was how strong the lenses were, strong enough to see in her lower lip the same pout as on the statue and the same pout as in Gabriella's photographs. Now I could recognize that all three pouts looked lazy while all three faces looked tight. Gabriella and Lois were one and the same. Kirsten had seen this right away.

Lois stepped through the missing board and crossed the Lazore backyard. She had a bucket of water and a scrub brush and spray-on soap. She started washing the face of the statue and then washed along the neck and then down the arms and then to the legs before kneeling to do the feet. She looked biblical, kneeling before the statue of herself.

Finished cleaning, she wandered about in the weeds, bending over, looking down, feeling for something in the grass, finally down on her hands and knees with what looked like a garden trowel trying to smooth away where Kirsten had dug.

The rats were the answer. I felt them scurrying up from the basement, filling my mind with the whispers of baby Isabela buried under the concrete, soon to be found, unlike the Speed River baby, who would never be found. But no. Maybe the feeling I was having was that Kirsten, when finished here, would find that other baby too. Of course, all these confused feelings were some kind of subconscious need to know that that baby was laid to rest somewhere, not lying botfly-covered and rotting on the river bank, and that was Kirsten's agenda with the flowers and the shovel as soon as she had finished her agenda here.

I found Kirsten in the hall examining with her flashlight the pictures of Isabela wrapped in a pink blanket and pink hat in her bassinet. Kirsten said to Isabela, "You're close by, and so are the other little girls, and so is Emily. Tell me where."

I found myself cocking my head, turning my ear, listening for the answer.

Chapter Twenty-Seven

I had left Kirsten communicating with the photographs and had gone to the corner for Tim Hortons. When I got back, I stood for a minute in the front yard of the Lazore, thinking, This is how "Adventures with Kirsten" got started. First, the Gabriella statue caught me in her line of sight and then she caught Kirsten in her line of sight and here we are, both of us ensnared.

I stepped back and looked up at the windows, two on the first floor and three on the second and one small attic window at the peak. I climbed the porch steps and knocked on the front door, but she didn't answer. I walked through the weeds to the back. I stepped into the kitchen. No Kirsten. The doors along the lower floor were shut, the hallway gloomy. I opened each door in turn, did a quick look-through, then climbed the stairs to the second floor, where the doors were all shut except the staircase to the attic, a room I had not investigated.

I started up a second set of stairs, narrower than the first, and stopped halfway when my eyes became level with the small point of light shining through the old-fashioned keyhole of the door at the top. Leaning forward to look through, I could see what appeared to be a bed and an end table. I stood at the door, listening, before easing my hand over the doorknob, which turned without a sound, and swung the door open.

Kirsten sat on the edge of the bed, holding her flashlight. I came into the attic room and, ducking my head for the slant of the rafters, went around to the far side. I said, "Parsons phoned. No doubt about it. It's the nanny. She's part of the same cartel as the first one. Trafficking is the second-largest illegal activity next to the drug trade. Eighty per cent of the victims are female. The woman gets phony citizenship papers and identity, gets a nanny job, tells the kid they're going to Disneyland, and delivers to the cartel the child in her care and then disappears, using fake passports to get back to their own country."

Kirsten seemed to be thinking about it, accepting it. Or maybe it was only me thinking about it, accepting it. I could never tell what was going on in her head. She was sitting in a sullen slouch, her hair teased into an intentional mess, the red fingernails resting in her lap, the painted toenails in one black sandal struggling with that one crooked toe.

I sat beside her and turned her head. "You've got a bruise there. Above your left eye. What happened?"

"It's nothing." She ran her finger over it. "The hurricane door came apart when I tried to open it. It's too heavy. I need your help."

"I'm glad to hear that. I was beginning to think you could do it all on your own. It's not easy having Superwoman as a partner."

"Superwoman has lost her powers. All I've got to show for my investigations is this. I used this thing when the drains got plugged. It's a drain snake. What I need is some psychic Drano."

She handed me the drain snake, a round plastic thing with the end of a thick wire poking out.

"You hold it like this and wheel out the wire into the drain and find out what's down there."

"What drain are you planning to snake?"

"I don't know yet. Nothing. I don't know. Maybe I'm done here. Maybe it's over."

A neighbour of the Ducks, Clem, had brought over a live rat and a re-wired electric toothbrush to see if Willie was interested in investing in a side business. When he plugged it in, the rat sitting on the workshop bench leaped in the air and dropped to the floor and scrambled into the corner.

Clem said, "The sound waves are so high frequency we can't hear them, but the screech almost blasts the rat's head off."

Clem looked like a mad scientist as he flipped the switch and the rat tried to climb the wall.

Clem said, "Calls work two ways. Ducks you want to come; rats you want to go. It will work better than poison. The stuff you buy at the store doesn't do nothing."

When the Ducks went to commercials, Kirsten said, "The Lazore is full of rats. The I Ching says rats have super fine-tuned hearing. They can hear secrets carried by whiffs of air from hundreds of years ago, and their noses can read sniffs of who and what has ever touched every surface of every doorknob in that spooky house. If you want to know something about the Lazore, you catch one of the rats and lean your ear close to its ear. It's like how when you listen to a seashell, you can hear waves from a hundred years ago crashing on some far-away beach. The rats can hear the sound of termites creeping through the walls. That's how in China they knew if their houses had termites. They could hear the rats in there catching the termites. The rats can hear people talking on the telephone lines along the street; they can hear the slippery crawling of dew worms in the grass in the front yard."

I said, "If you're going to ask me to catch one for you so you can watch its nose sniffing out long-ago smells and watch its ears twitching at the long-ago noises and hold that rat up to my ear close enough that it can it whisper all its secrets to me, I don't think I want to do that, thanks all the same give your head a shake."

"In Haiti, the rats know when a hurricane is coming and they head for high ground. They can hear the wind building up fifty miles away, the same as they can hear sounds from fifty years ago. We sit here not hearing anything, but the rats can hear sounds from way back when the first people lived here: the *crunch-crunch* of some long-ago wife seated at the kitchen table eating her cucumber sandwich; the footsteps of the long-ago husband on the front walk arriving home from work; the rattle of the long-ago postman at the mailbox."

"And let me guess, the crying of the long-ago baby in her crib."

"You're catching on, dude."

Next morning, I was opening the hurricane doors and stepping into the sudden chilly dampness of the Lazore basement. My job: catch a rat. Kirsten led the way, flashlight in one hand, the other against the cold stone wall.

She pressed the flashlight switch. "Damn. Why didn't I check the batteries?" She sat on the third step. "No lights and a flashlight with dead batteries." She searched through her purse. "The bathroom trick Aunt Bessie taught me."

The flame from the match flickered in the draft drawing up from inside as we stepped into the dead black silence.

Kirsten lit another match. She moved some boxes aside and slid her sandaled feet along the concrete floor to a door, held shut by a hook and eye. As she pulled it open, the rasping screech of the hinges burst from the blackness and a rush of warm air brought the smell of burnt cookies.

She led the way, following the current. "That's all we need to do, like a butterfly riding the wind all the way to that place in Mexico."

The match blinked out. We crept in slow steps along the concrete to another open door. In the pitch black, I could hear a faint buzzing. A third match lighting the shadowy grey took us to a corner where more boxes were piled. I moved them aside. Feeling along the damp wall, I found a second door, also held shut by a hook and eye. Again, the rasping screech of the hinges burst from the blackness as the warm air rushed through the whirled spiderwebs that hung across the opening.

I saw another corridor leading into the darkness. Kirsten pushed ahead through the cobwebs and we followed the passage until it dead-ended at another concrete wall. A second corridor led left and right. Now we could hear a high-pitched buzzing that seemed to come from our left. We continued one step after another as the air grew heavier, and the tunnel became so black that her fourth match barely showed her other hand groping her way forward. We turned back and took the other corridor with the fresher air until, rounding a corner, we saw a ray of light filtering through the dusty window of a small room.

When we entered the doorway, swarms of buzzing insects swelled up in clouds from the shadows, forcing us to stumble backward, swatting them, brushing them off our skin, out of our hair, until, realizing we had not been stung, we returned to the doorway. As soon as we stepped inside, the insects came alive again, flying up in clouds, landing on our clothes and our hair.

"Botflies," she said, waving them away and going into the room.

On the far wall, high up, a window looked into the front yard. I felt around the frame, hoping it might open, but no luck. I found a spot near the window to sit down, next to a pile of discarded furnace ducts and plumbing pipes.

I said, "Here we are, 'Adventures with Kirsten.'"

I settled myself with my back against the stone foundation wall. I tried to think of what to do. In the dark, we would eventually find our way back to the hurricane doors. But easier would be to smash out the window and hoist Kirsten through so she could go to the store and buy batteries.

As I struggled to my feet, coming up from all fours, my eyes were drawn to the line of dust floating in the faint light from the window. When I looked through the glass, I saw the statue, and I saw that Gabriella's line of sight was following this dusty diagonal into the pile of furnace ducts and plumbing pipes in the far corner.

Chapter Twenty-Eight

Flashing in an arc across the concrete floor and up the stone wall, a beam of light moved without a sound from the shadows, sliding along the concrete toward us. I took Kirsten's hand and we crouched behind the ducts and waited as the funnel swept into the room and arced once around its perimeters.

Lois stood by the window, looking out. She turned and gazed into the room. "Wherever you are, Isabela, come out, come out."

Our movements behind the pipes must have stirred up some dust, for I felt a sneeze trying to break out from the base of my nose. I pinched my nostrils, holding it back as Lois turned from the window and came our way. Her light slid back and forth, lighting up our hiding place so brightly that I was waiting for her to say, "There you are, Isabela."

But the light flared off to the other corner as she turned away and left.

Finally, certain Lois must be gone, I placed my hands on the floor to ease myself up from the pipes without making a racket. I turned to help Kirsten but she was busy with something caught in one sandal. I knelt to look. A thin slice of concrete was wedged under the crooked big toe. I felt along the floor. Chunks were breaking away from a crack buried beneath the pipes. Poking about with my fingers, I discovered the concrete was coming away in thin slabs from a jagged hole about five inches across.

Kirsten yoga-squatted on the floor and stared at the hole. "The answer to the question 'Where is Isabela' is down that hole. I know it. It's like she's holding a slip of paper in her hand, trying to stick it up out of the hole like a sign; 'Here I am.'"

I heard a scrape and scuttle of claws. I bent close to the opening to listen but heard nothing. Then from inside the tunnel, I heard the scratching of claws as they came piling out, one after another, falling over one another, squeaking and chattering so loudly Kirsten held her hands over his ears. In the mouth of the biggest rat, that now sat staring straight at her, was a tiny bone.

It scurried aside, well away from the hole. A second rat began to claw away the broken pieces of cement and dig into the dirt, finally uncovering another larger bone. I picked up a slice of concrete and threw it sideways, almost cutting off the rat's legs as it scrambled across the floor and scrambled to the corner and slipped away, from there probably into another hole leading to another cavity, and maybe a second opening leading to another opening directly into a groundhog hole.

She picked up the tiny bones and took them to the light.

I said, "Give them to Parsons."

"Are you kidding? He'll put up the yellow tape. He's part of the problem."

Chapter Twenty-Nine

We were so close to the end, I could feel it. I knew by the end of the day I would be saying goodbye to the Lazore family, telling Dr. Lazore that playing detective with Kirsten in his haunted rat-filled house had been a trying experience, like now, leaning on a shovel, the statue of Gabriella looking at me like a wingless angel in an abandoned graveyard waiting to see what I would do next.

I stepped away from the statue and stood back and looked at the Lazore from the street, hovering in the twilight shadows. I imagined the Lazore going backward, coming to life, the two Lazore upper-level lights snapping on, first one then the other. I imagined the Lazore living room light snapping on as the street lights came to life, lifting Gabriella out of the shadows, and bringing her back to life, seated in the living room with mother and father and baby, a happy scene.

I turned to look at the statue. In the mix of light and dark, I saw that Gabriella's eyes seemed bi-coloured but I could not make out what the colours were. As I approached the statue, I saw a movement of brown. At first, I thought it was the street lights moving the shadows around. Then I saw a rat scamper along the edge of the Lazore foundation and disappear into the weeds of the backyard. It reappeared by the board fence. It sat there, waiting for me it seemed.

I went over to stand beside Kirsten, snake in hand, ready to explore the groundhog hole. She was watching the rat who was watching her.

"Did you want me to catch it?"

It disappeared into the shadows and then reappeared three feet away, watching us, little nose leaning forward for a better sniff. Kirsten took a few steps closer, softly chanting, "Where are those other little girls, Mr. Rat? Mr. Rat, where are the little girls?" casting her spell on the rat like she cast her spell on Lenssen and me and the reverend.

The lights blinked on in Lois's kitchen window. Below the window, I saw Kirsten's new rat friend disappear into a sliver of light coming from a crack in Lois's foundation. When I took a step forward, the sliver vanished. A step backward, no sliver. Only in this one spot, directly facing the direction the rat had gone, was light visible.

I ducked down to lean one-eyed for a closer look through that crack, but I could see nothing. I skirted the house, hoping for a lit basement window, but they all seemed covered from the inside. I stood in the weeds at one corner of the house. Looking one way, I could see the street lights in front of Lois's house, and looking the other way, I could see the street lights in front of the Lazore. I remembered Kirsten sitting at my kitchen table reading to me what I then considered nonsense from the I Ching, something about studying the bone patterns of the chicken we'd just finished eating. She'd boiled them into soup stock, dried them out, and arranged them according to the master's instructions.

Crazy as reading those Tarot cards. No different from predicting your future from reading the cosmic planetary pattern presenting itself in a six-topping pizza. I glanced at her, standing with her back to the Lazore but facing the statue, waiting for a message from Mr. Rat. Or from those little bones now in her pocket, poking into her thighs, telling her what direction to take. Maybe those bones were working like antennae, picking up gravitational forces from her planetary messengers.

Kirsten came over. "I have the answer. The stonemason, Arnie, said the concrete slab the statue is sitting on is eight feet by eight feet wide. But that statue is off-centre. When I was digging at the base of the statue, my shovel went into dirt. That slab has sunk over time and has been filling over with dirt. Lois would want the little girls buried under the concrete like Isabela. The radar couldn't find them because she buried them tucked away underneath the slab of concrete, a hollowed-out grave for them to nestle in."

I was waiting for her to give me instructions to start digging when I noticed the glint of light again. It seemed to be glancing off one large foundation rock, like maybe a vein of quartz or mica or whatever the names of the minerals that sparkled were. Kirsten came over and knelt and removed some smaller rocks. Then, using the drain snake, she opened a peephole. Now I could see that between the foundation and the inside wall was a layer of pink insulation. Kirsten crouched down on her knees and twisted the snake into the insulation and through the drywall to open a hole big enough to peek through. On hands and knees, I crouched beside her. I saw the back of a chair, and beside the chair, a mattress with blankets neatly made up. It looked like this bed was waiting for someone to climb under its covers. By crouching low to the ground, I was able to climb my vision upwards from the chair.

Lois seemed smaller, her face tighter from this angle. She was talking to someone. I could not hear the words but I could see from the facial gestures that Lois was agitated. Her hands on the back of the chair were white-knuckled as a sobbing Emily took her place at the little table, set with a dish of what looked like red Jell-O.

Lois lifted one hand off the chair to wag a finger at the crying child. Lois looked worn out. She looked like she wanted to lie down on the mattress. She seemed to be saying, I am tired of your crying and my mind is about to snap.

Back at the iron fence, dialing 911, I waited for what was coming which, when it came, was not "I told you so, dude." It was "Thank God. We found her."

Chapter Thirty

I stood by the iron fence watching the backhoe digging up the Lazore yard. Kirsten stood a few feet off, conning Parsons into not charging her with interfering with a police investigation. "I admit I broke into the Lazore, but the seed that had been planted refused to stop growing, especially after I noticed the dead smell coming from the basement."

"Dead smell?"

She said, "Quinn asked me, 'Kirsten, why are you spending so much time at the Lazore? What are you up to? You need to stay out of the Emily investigation and mind your own business.' So I told him about the smell, like burnt cookies."

Parsons said, "Back to the beginning: you rented Quinn's apartment and then you decided you wanted to be a detective like him?"

"I wanted to get to know him. That's how you get to know people. You make up an activity, like going bowling."

Parsons pointed his thumb in my direction. "You wanted *him* to go bowling?"

"It's not about bowling. It's about getting to know people, about connecting. But he doesn't do any activities. He sits at home and watches the Ducks and the next day he goes to work. So, I had to make up an activity."

"Hard to picture Quinn going bowling."

"A better example: we got a shovel and went together to the Lazore to work side by side, you know, working in the soil, planting flowers. It makes you think about getting back to your roots; maybe our grandparents were farmers. As I laboured in the field and Quinn laboured in the field, we would both get the urge to talk about our relatives that must have laboured in the fields, and so on."

Parsons said, "I still don't get it. Why did you want to get to know him?"

"I thought we had some history in common. You know, you meet someone and this and that and you begin to wonder and well, you know you get feelings..."

Parsons was not writing anything down so I knew there would be no charges.

Me and Kirsten stood by the statue watching the JCB junior backhoe dig up Gabriella's graveyard: so far ten rag dolls and three bodies, the remains carefully lifted and bagged by forensics. Isabela was found right where Kirsten said, under five inches of concrete in the Lazore's basement.

It was a hot morning in late June. I took off my suit jacket and folded it over the iron-rail fence. I thought that, while the backhoe was there, they would knock down the statue that now leaned at more of a tilt from the excavation. But that would take a court order and endless delays and miles of tape both yellow and red, and in the end it would fall over anyway, or be knocked over by the neighbours.

Kirsten was staring at the dug-up Lazore yard, her forehead covered in sweat and filled with frown lines. She said, "Digging up the graves, turning over the soil, it's like turning the cross right-side up." Then she added, "I wonder what Aunt Bessie would say if she could see me now."

I wondered about Aunt Bessie. My father had had a car he called Bessie. My great uncle had had a draft horse called Bessie that he used for skidding logs out of the bush. There was Bessie the cow. The one day I met a woman named Bessie, I remembered thinking, I didn't know people were actually called Bessie.

I asked Kirsten, "Do you have an actual Aunt Bessie or did you make her up?"

The backhoe continued to dig. The sun was hot. No breeze in the yard. I was beginning to sweat, although, like the city workers leaning on their shovels, I was doing no work.

Kirsten said, "There's something karmic about digging. You listen for years to the clean rasping sound of the shovel slicing into the dirt. Then one day, right about the time you've given up digging and thrown the shovel aside, because to heck with it, you bend down and look and right before your eyes, a seed that got planted years ago becomes a rose suddenly blooming."

"Kirsten. For me, it's this or it's that. Either you tell me or you don't, but stop playing games."

Kirsten shifted down to sit cross-legged in the weeds. She settled herself and pulled her knees up and rested her head on her arms. She straightened up. She said, "Sit down beside me, Quinn. Don't worry about your nice suit pants. Sit here with me in the weeds. When we get home, I'll throw the pants into the laundry, spray them with stain remover, take them to the cleaners, get you a new pair for ten dollars at the thrift shop, whatever."

I sat where she pointed.

She was frowning at the Lazore, looking as sad as it did.

"Aunt Bessie liked motorcycles. She liked to hear the wind blowing through her hair. I thought that was so cool. All my twelve-year-old girlfriends were getting their ears pierced but I said no. I thought it would change the sound of the wind blowing through my hair if I ever got the chance to ride a motorcycle. But eventually I gave in and had them pierced anyway."

Her face was flushed and sweaty from the sun. A slight breeze would have returned her to her normal Kirsten look. But there was none.

"Aunt Bessie said, 'People do all kinds of things to their ears; pierce holes in them and hang stuff on them, like a Christmas tree that you throw away. They wear headphones over them and blast their eardrums with dynamite music. The bikers on their Harleys knock the baffles out of their mufflers the same as they knock the baffles out of their heads.' So Aunt Bessie made sure I looked after my hearing."

She took my finger. "Feel my ear."

I ran the tip of my finger along the edge of her ear.

"The ear is a miracle just like the brain is a miracle. Feel my sweaty forehead." She took my hand and placed it on her forehead. "But this miracle brain and these miracle ears have been working overtime. They need a rest. So, I'm telling you now because I'm running out of energy: the game has worn me out."

She folded her legs up into a yoga pose and said, "You feel my forehead but you can't feel what's in there that allows me to think and to understand any more than you can feel when you touch my ear what's in there that allows me to hear and understand."

She gave me back my hand.

"We've all got noises in our heads, but they're silenced by baffles. If you take the baffles out, you get my mother. Aunt Bessie told me my father tried to help my mother get her life straight, but he gave up. In fact, now that I've been talking about baffles and mufflers, I seem to remember you smelled like exhaust fumes. Maybe from sitting in your police car on stake-outs. But I don't know. I was just a baby.

"I looked at the statue. Its eyes were saying, 'Dig it up, Kirsten, lay it down, and take a closer look.' I looked at Lois standing at her kitchen window. Her eyes were saying, 'Dig it up, Kirsten, lay it down and take a closer look.'"

Kirsten continued. "My mother had fallen and was trying to get back on her feet and stand up straight and there you were to help. I got the photograph. I can show you, standing there looking at me in my pink bonnet and pink snuggy like Isabela in her pink bassinet. You looked like you didn't know what to do with me. You reached down and touched my big toe. Aunt Bessie explained, 'Men don't know what to do with babies so they just stand there looking stupid, or they do something stupid, like touch the big toe.'"

I looked at the toe. Kirsten had had such small feet then, and there they were now, in their sandals with the toenails a shiny red, the big one I had touched gone a little crooked.

"What I'm trying to say, dude, is… It's like a policeman gets into a situation and shoots a dog. Just happens. Everyone gets upset that the policeman shot a dog. The dog lovers want an inquiry. The Humane Society launches a lawsuit. The television cameras go to the house of the dog person. Cry me a river. But what if the story gets the attention of someone not even interested in dogs, just sitting there in her apartment watching the news, totally unconnected. Probably nothing. But what if one day it's not a shot dog, it's a drowning baby. What if for that person a memory gets jogged, and a chain of events is set off, because that someone has needed to remedy a few things, not about a dog but about a baby.

"I couldn't just land on your doorstep and say, 'I'm your daughter.' A gazillion things could go wrong; like with anything I do, something would go wrong. There might have been a better way to do what I had to do, but I needed to do it, like get things remedied — nothing specific, this or that — and so a daughter turns up on your doorstep, the strangest thing."

I nodded, "Strangest thing…"

"I saw right away that when you looked at me, you saw my mother. So, I thought, if that's the hook then let's set the line. But this has left me with a head full of I-did-it-all-wrong thoughts running like an IV drip from the saline bag into my subconscious and into my veins and into my mind and back into the bag. That's what it feels like when you fret about all the things you did wrong. Because you see, dude, although it was 'Adventures with Kirsten' for you, it was 'Reality with Quinn' for me.

"Aunt Bessie told me she and my mother never met their father. She said my mother used to wonder what would happen if he came into whatever strip club she was working at and they wouldn't recognize one another until they were up in the VIP. How would that feel? Or she used to wonder, what if she wanted to straighten her life out and she needed help and she thought this father whom she'd never met could help her? But how could she make that work? She couldn't come up to his door and say, 'I'm your daughter and I'm a stripper and my life is a mess and I need your help.'

"So how could I land on your doorstep and say, 'I'm a barmaid and my life is a mess and I need your help?' So, I needed a way to show you I was a decent person, but first I needed to get you interested in my plan, so yeah, I admit being a flirt was not the best way to do it, and that's the part I regret."

Kirsten looked down at herself. "You have to admit, it got your attention, although there might have been a better way to make good on those intentions, which was to force you into getting to know me before I said, 'Guess what, I'm your daughter.'

"After they showed the news clip about the baby in the river, they showed the ShamWow guy commercial, with the thirty-day free trial and money back guaranteed, all for some kind of magic sponge. First I thought, 'How can I get a free trial and then get my money back if I don't like the product?' Then I thought, 'How can I keep his attention long enough for him to get to know the product?' Then the ShamWow guy got a new commercial, you know, the one where he does the onion dicer. He says, 'So they're making you cry and well they're making me cry and life is hard enough without needing to cry over a vegetable.'

"I had become haunted by the ghost of a father who I was afraid would turn into an onion and make me cry. But I had to give it a shot and I did. And you turned out to be a vegetable I liked. But then, just when I was going to tell you the truth, you told me to move. You didn't want me. That felt like me wanting to keep the ShamWow sponge and the onion dicer but the ShamWow guy wanting them back."

Kirsten sighed deeply. "For me, the sky was dark and cloudy and the lightning was flashing and the wind was whistling and the windows were shadowy and I broke into your life like I broke into the Lazore. So here we are, the perfect picture, father and daughter, me leaning into you, the sun shining upon us both."

She looked up at me, waiting. "Is there anything happening in that brain, Detective, or has the cat got your baffles?"

I was remembering. My first year as detective twenty-four years ago, staking out strip clubs for drugs. Carmen was renting the ground floor of an old house on Shuter Street. I gave her money for groceries, took her to Tim Hortons a few times, but that was about all I had done. She had no idea which biker was the father of this baby, but she wanted to be able to tell her daughter her father was someone decent.

I remembered that she was sitting on the bed, staring at the floor. She had said, "I don't mean for now. But maybe for later, can I lie to the kid and say her father was this really nice detective, not one of those biker morons."

Kirsten took my big hand in her two small hands. "You're not an onion, dude. You're the father I've always wanted: built to fight but born to love."

I remembered the day I had first noticed the Gabriella statue, staring at me from the shadows, from one angle saying, 'Stay out,' and from another angle saying, 'Come in.' It was like the statue was saying, 'On the one hand, you're better off leaving buried babies buried, and on the other hand, maybe you need to dig them up.'

It seemed to me like I'd been sitting like this in the weeds forever. It seemed to me it was time to put my big left arm around Kirsten's small shoulders and hold her. When I did, I was surprised at how tiny and delicate she was.

"Are you with me, dude? Blink if your ears are still working. If you have anything to say, say it. Because, dude, now is the time to separate the facts from the assumptions and the hopes from the feelings."

I said, "I was just thinking about changing the name of the agency to Quinn and Quinn."

Kirsten said, "I'm not sure I want to catch cheaters though. I'm not sure cheaters should be caught. Better to let them work through whatever the cheating is about before they get caught."

Her face became thoughtful. "But I don't know. Sometimes a woman would come into the bar and have a few and say, 'My husband died a week ago,' and I would say, 'Oh I'm sorry,' and she would say, 'Don't be. I'm glad to see the end of him. The best thing that ever happened to me.' Which is what I'm saying now. You're the best thing that ever happened to me."

www.ingramcontent.com/pod-product-compliance
Lightning Source LLC
Chambersburg PA
CBHW021232020726
47498CB00008B/2803